'So you won't give this baby up and neither will I,' Ariston said softly. 'Which means that the only solution is to marry.'

He saw the shock and horror on Keeley's face.

'But I don't want to marry you! It wouldn't work, Ariston—on so many levels. You must realise that. Me as the wife of an autocratic control-freak who doesn't even like me? I don't think so.'

'It wasn't a question,' he said silkily. 'It was a statement. It's not a case of *if* you will marry me, Keeley—just when.'

One Night With Consequences

When one night…leads to pregnancy!

When succumbing to a night of unbridled desire
it's impossible to think past the morning after!

But, with the sheets barely settled, that little blue line
appears on the pregnancy test and it doesn't take long
to realise that one night of white-hot passion
has turned into a lifetime of consequences!

Only one question remains:

How do you tell a man you've just met
that you're about to share more than just his bed?

Find out in:

An Heir to Make A Marriage by Abby Green

The Greek's Nine-Month Redemption by Maisey Yates

Crowned for the Prince's Heir by Sharon Kendrick

The Sheikh's Baby Scandal by Carol Marinelli

A Ring for Vincenzo's Heir by Jennie Lucas

Claiming His Christmas Consequence by Michelle Smart

The Guardian's Virgin Ward by Caitlin Crews

A Child Claimed by Gold by Rachael Thomas

The Consequence of His Vengeance by Jennie Lucas

Secrets of a Billionaire's Mistress by Sharon Kendrick

The Boss's Nine-Month Negotiation by Maya Blake

Look for more **One Night With Consequences** stories
coming soon!

THE PREGNANT KAVAKOS BRIDE

BY
SHARON KENDRICK

First Published in Great Britain 2017
By Mills & Boon, an imprint of HarperCollins*Publishers*
1 London Bridge Street, London, SE1 9GF

ISBN: 978-0-263-92443-5

Sharon Kendrick once won a national writing competition by describing her ideal date: being flown to an exotic island by a gorgeous and powerful man. Little did she realise that she'd just wandered into her dream job! Today she writes for Mills & Boon, featuring often stubborn but always *to die for* heroes and the women who bring them to their knees. She believes that the best books are those you never want to end. Just like life…

Visit the Author Profile page
at millsandboon.co.uk for more titles.

For the ever-amusing Amelia Tuttiett,
who is a brilliant ceramicist and an inspirational teacher.

CHAPTER ONE

SHE WAS EVERYTHING he hated about a woman and she was talking to his brother. Ariston Kavakos grew very still as he stared at her. At curves guaranteed to make a man desire her whether he wanted to or not. And he most definitely did not. Yet his body was stubbornly refusing to obey the dictates of his mind and a powerful shaft of lust arrowed straight to his groin.

Who the hell had invited Keeley Turner?

She was standing close to Pavlos, her blonde hair rippling beneath the overhead lights of the swish London art gallery. She lifted her hand as if to emphasise a point and Ariston found his gaze drawn to the most amazing breasts he had ever seen. He swallowed as he remembered her in a dripping wet bikini with rivulets of water trickling down over her belly as she emerged from the foamy blue waters of the Aegean. She was memory and fantasy all mixed up in one. Something started and never finished. Eight years on and Keeley Turner made him want to look at her and only her, despite the stunning photographs of his private Greek island which dominated the walls of the London gallery.

Was his brother similarly smitten? He hoped not, although it was hard to tell because their body language excluded the rest of the world as they stood deep in conversation. Ariston began to walk across the gallery but if they noticed him approach they chose not to acknowledge it. He felt a flicker of rage, which he quickly cast aside because rage could be counterproductive. He knew that now. Icy calm was far more effective in dealing with difficult situations and it had been the key to his success. The means by which he had dragged his family's ailing company out of the dust and built it anew and gained a reputation of being the man with the Midas touch. The dissolute reign of his father was over and his elder son was now firmly in charge. These days the Kavakos shipping business was the most profitable on the planet and he intended to keep it that way.

His mouth hardened. Which meant more than just dealing with shipbrokers and being up to speed with the state of world politics. It meant keeping an eye on the more gullible members of the family. Because there was a lot of money sloshing around the Kavakos empire and he knew how women acted around money. An early lesson in feminine greed had changed his life for ever and that was why he never took his eye off the ball. His attitude meant that some people considered him controlling, but Ariston preferred to think of himself as a guiding influence—like a captain steering a ship. And in a way, life *was* like being at sea. You steered clear of icebergs for obvious reasons and women were like icebergs. You only ever saw ten per cent of what they were *really* like—the rest was buried deep beneath the self-serving and grasping surface.

His eyes didn't leave the blonde as he walked towards them, knowing that if she was going to be a problem in his brother's life he would deal with it—and quickly. His lips curved into the briefest of smiles. He would have her dispatched before she even realised what was happening.

'Why, Pavlos,' Ariston said softly as he reached them and he noticed that the woman had instantly grown tense. 'This *is* a surprise. I wasn't expecting to see you here so soon after the opening night. Have you developed a late-onset love of photography or are you just homesick for the island on which you were born?'

Pavlos didn't look too happy to be interrupted—but Ariston didn't care. Right then he couldn't think about anything except what was happening inside him. Because, infuriatingly, he seemed to have developed no immunity against the green-eyed temptress he'd last seen when she was eighteen, when she'd thrown herself at him with a hunger which had blown his mind. Her submission had been instant and would have been total if he hadn't put a stop to it. Displaying the sexist double standards for which he had occasionally been accused, he had despised her availability at the same time as he'd been bewitched by it. It had taken all his legendary self-control to push her away and to adjust his clothing but he had done it, though it had left him hard and aching for what had seemed like months afterwards. His mouth tightened because she was nothing but a tramp. A cheap and grasping little tramp.

Like mother, like daughter, he thought grimly—and the last type of woman he wanted his brother getting mixed up with.

'Oh, hi, Ariston,' said Pavlos with the easy manner which made most people surprised when they learned they were brothers. 'That's right, here I am again. I decided to pay a second visit and meet up with an old friend at the same time. You remember Keeley, don't you?'

There was a moment of silence while a pair of bright green eyes were lifted to his and Ariston felt the loud hammer of his heart.

'Of course I remember Keeley,' he said roughly, aware of the irony of his words. Because for him most women *were* forgettable and nothing more than a means to an end. Oh, sometimes he might recall a pair of spectacular breasts or a pert bottom—or if a woman was especially talented with her lips or hands, she might occasionally merit a nostalgic smile. But Keeley Turner had been in a class of her own and he'd never been able to shift her from the corners of his mind. Because she'd been off-limits and forbidden? Or because she had given him a taste of unbelievable sweetness before he'd forced himself to reject her? Ariston didn't know. It was as inexplicable as it was powerful and he found himself studying her with the same intensity as the nearby people peering at the photos which adorned the gallery walls.

Petite yet impossibly curvy, her thick hair hung down her back in a curtain of pale and rippling waves. Her jeans were ordinary and her thin sweater unremarkable yet somehow that didn't seem to matter. With a body like hers she could have worn a piece of sackcloth and still looked like dynamite. The cheap, man-made fabric strained over the lushness of her breasts and the blue denim caressed the curves of her bottom. Her mouth was bare of lipstick and her eyes wore only a lick of mascara as they studied him warily. Hers was not a modern look—yet there was something about Keeley Turner... An indefinable something which touched a sensual core deep inside him and made him want to peel her clothes from her body and ride her until she was screaming his name. But he wanted her gone more than he wanted to bed her—and maybe he should set about accomplishing that right now.

Deliberately excluding her from the conversation, Ariston turned to his brother and summoned up a bland smile. 'I wasn't aware you two were friends.'

'We haven't actually seen each other for years,' said Pavlos. 'Not since that holiday.'

'I suspect that holiday is an event which none of us particularly care to revisit,' said Ariston smoothly, enjoying the sudden rush of colour which had made her cheeks turn a deep shade of pink. 'Yet you've stayed in touch with each other all this time?'

'We're friends on social media,' Pavlos elaborated, with a shrug. 'You know how it is.'

'Actually, I don't. You know my views on social media and none of them are positive.' Ariston made no attempt to hide his frosty disapproval. 'I need to talk to you, Pavlos. Alone,' he added.

Pavlos frowned. 'When?'

'Now.'

'But I've only just met up with Keeley. Can't it wait?'

'I'm afraid it can't.' He saw Pavlos shoot her an apologetic glance as if to apologise for his brother's bullish behaviour but social niceties didn't bother him. He'd worked hard for most of his life to ensure that Pavlos was kept away from the kind of scandals which had once engulfed their family. He'd been determined he wouldn't go the same sorry way as their father. He'd made sure that he'd attended a good boarding school in England and a university in Switzerland, and he had carefully influenced his choice of friends—and girl-friends. And this pretty little tramp in her cheap dress and come-to-bed eyes was about to learn that his baby brother was strictly off-limits. 'It's business,' he added firmly.

'Not more trouble in the Gulf?'

'Something like that,' Ariston agreed, irritated at his brother's attitude and wondering why he'd forgotten you didn't talk family business in front of strangers. 'We can use one of the offices here at the gallery—they're very accommodating,' he added smoothly. 'The owner is a friend of mine.'

'But Keeley—'

'Oh, don't worry about Keeley. I'm sure she has the imagination to take care of herself. There's plenty for her to look at.' Ariston turned to give her a hard version of a smile, noticing that her knuckles had suddenly whitened as she clutched her thin shawl. For the first time he spoke directly to her, dropping his voice to a silken murmur which his business rivals would have recognised as being a tone you didn't mess with. 'And plenty of men hanging around who would be all too happy to take my brother's place. In fact, I can see a couple watching you right now. I'm sure you could have a lot of fun with them, Keeley. You really mustn't let us keep you any longer.'

Keeley felt her face freeze as Ariston spoke to her, wishing she could come up with a suitably crushing response to throw at the powerful Greek who was looking at her as if she was a stain on the pale floorboards and talking to her as if she was some kind of hooker. But the truth was that she didn't *trust* herself to speak— afraid that her words would come out as meaningless babble. Because that was the effect he had on her. The effect he had on all women. Even when he was talking to them—or should she say *at* them?—with utter contempt in his eyes, he could reduce them to a level of longing which wasn't like the stuff you felt around most men. He could make you have fantasies about him, even though he exuded nothing but darkness.

She'd seen the way her own mother had looked at him. She could see the other women in the gallery watching him now—their gazes hungry but wary—as if they were observing a different type of species and weren't sure how to handle him. As if they realised they should stay well away but were itching to touch him all the same. And she could hardly judge them for that, could she? Because hadn't *she* flung herself at him? Pressed her body hard against his and longed for him to take away the aching deep inside her. Behaved like a cheap little fool by misinterpreting a simple gesture on his part and managing to make a bad situation even worse.

The last time she'd seen him her life had pretty much imploded and eight years later she was still dealing with the fallout. Keeley's mouth tightened. Because she'd come through far too much to let the arrogant billionaire make her feel bad about herself. She suspected that the mocking challenge sparking from his blue eyes was intended to make her excuse herself and disappear, but she wasn't going to do that. A quiet rebellion began to build inside her. Did he really think he had the power to kick her out of this public gallery, as once he had kicked her off his private island?

'I wasn't planning on going anywhere,' she said, seeing his eyes darken with anger. 'I'm quite happy looking at photographs of Lasia. I'd forgotten just what a beautiful island it was and I can certainly keep myself occupied until you get back.' She smiled. 'I'll wait here for you, Pavlos. Take as long as you like.'

It clearly wasn't the response Ariston wanted and she saw the irritation which hardened his beautiful features.

'As you wish,' he said tightly. 'Though I cannot guarantee how long we'll be.'

She met his cold blue stare with a careless smile. 'Don't worry about it. I'm not in any hurry.'

He shrugged. 'Very well. Come, Pavlos.'

He began to walk away with his brother by his side and, although she told herself to look away, Keeley could do nothing but stand and stare, just like everyone else in the gallery.

She'd forgotten how tall and rugged he was because she had *forced* herself to forget—to purge her memory of a sensuality which had affected her like no other. But now it was all coming back. The olive skin and tendrils of hair which brushed so blackly against his shirt collar. Yet she thought he seemed uncomfortable in the exquisite grey suit he wore. His muscular body looked constrained—as if he was more at home wearing the sawn-off denims he'd worn on Lasia. The ones which had emphasised his powerful thighs as he'd dived deep into the sapphire waters surrounding his island home. And it suddenly occurred to her that it didn't matter what he wore or what he said because nothing had changed. Not really. You saw him and you wanted him, it was as simple as that. She thought how cruel life could be—as if she needed any reminding—that the only man she'd ever desired was someone who made no secret about despising her.

With an effort, she tore her gaze away and forced herself to focus on a photograph which showed the island which had been in the Kavakos family for generations. Lasia was known as the paradise of the Cyclades with good reason and Keeley had felt as if she'd tumbled into paradise the moment she'd first set foot on its silvery sands. She had explored its surprisingly lush interior with delight until her mother's startling fall from grace had led to their visit being cut brutally short. She would never forget the hordes of press and the flash of cameras in their faces as they'd alighted from the boat which had taken them back to Piraeus. Or the screaming headlines when they'd arrived back in England—

and the cringe-making interviews her mother had given afterwards, which had only made matters worse. Keeley had been tainted by the scandal—an unwilling victim of circumstances beyond her control—and the knock-on effect had continued to this day.

Wasn't it that which had made her come here this afternoon—to meet up with Pavlos and remind herself of the beauty of the place? As if by doing that she could draw a line under the past and have some kind of closure? She'd hoped she might be able to eradicate some of the awful memories and replace them with better ones. She'd seen a picture of Ariston in the paper, attending the opening night, with some gorgeous redhead clinging like a vine to his arm. She certainly hadn't expected him to show up here today. Would she have come if she had known?

Of course she wouldn't. She wouldn't have set foot within a million miles of the place.

'Keeley?'

She turned around to find that Pavlos was back—with Ariston standing slightly behind him, not bothering to disguise the triumph curving his lips as his gaze clashed with hers.

'Hi,' she said, aware that the blue burn of his eyes was making her skin grow hot. 'You weren't long.'

A look of regret passed over Pavlos's face and somehow Keeley knew what was coming.

'No. I know I wasn't. Look, I'm afraid I'm going to have to bail out, Keeley,' he said. 'And take a rain check. Ariston needs me to fly out to the Middle East and take care of a ship.'

'What, now?' questioned Keeley, before she could stop herself.

'This very second,' put in Ariston silkily before adding, 'Should he have checked with you first?'

Pavlos bent to brush a brief kiss over each of her cheeks before giving her a quick smile. 'I'll message you later. Okay?'

'Sure.' She stood and watched him leave, aware that Ariston was still standing behind her but not trusting herself even to look at him. Instead, she tried very hard to concentrate on the photo she'd been studying—a sheltered bay where you could just make out shapes of giant turtles swimming in the crystal-clear waters. Perhaps he might just take the hint and go away. Leave her alone so that she could get to work on forgetting him all over again.

'I can't quite work out whether you are completely oblivious to my presence,' he said, in his dark, accented voice, 'or whether you just get a kick out of ignoring me.'

He had moved closer to stand beside her and Keeley lifted her gaze to find herself caught in that piercing sapphire stare and the resulting rush of blood went straight to her head. And her breasts. She could feel them become heavy and aching as the slow beat of her blood engorged them. Her mouth dried. How did he *do* that? Her fingers had grown numb and she was feeling almost dizzy but somehow she managed to compose a cool sentence. 'Why, do women always notice you whenever you walk into a room?'

'What do you think?'

And it was then that Keeley realised that she didn't have to play this game. Or *any* game. He was nothing to her. Nothing. *So stop acting like he's got some kind of power over you.* Yes, she'd once made a stupid mistake—but so what? It was a long time ago. She'd been young and stupid and she'd paid her dues—not to him, but to the universe—and *she didn't owe him anything.* Not even politeness.

'Honestly?' She gave a short laugh. 'I think you're unbelievably rude and arrogant, as well as having the most over-inflated ego of any man I've ever met.'

He raised his brows. 'And I imagine you must have met quite a few in your time.'

'Nowhere near the amount of women *you* must have notched up, if the papers are to be believed.'

'I don't deny it—but if you try to play the numbers game I'm afraid you'll never win.' His eyes glittered. 'Didn't anyone ever tell you that the rules for men and the rules for women are very different, *koukla mou*?'

'Only in the outdated universe you seem to occupy.'

He gave a careless shrug. 'It may not be fair but I'm afraid it's a fact of life. And men are allowed to behave in a way which would be disapproved of in a woman.'

His voice had dipped into a velvety caress and it was having precisely the wrong effect on her. Keeley could feel a hot flush of colour flooding into her cheeks as she made to move away.

'Let me pass, please,' she said, trying to keep her voice steady. 'I don't have to stand here and listen to this kind of Neanderthal...*rubbish.*'

'No, you're right. You don't.' He placed a restraining hand on her forearm. 'But before you go, maybe this is the ideal opportunity to get a few things straight between us.'

'What kind of things?'

'I think you know what I'm talking about, Keeley.'

'I'm afraid you've lost me.' She shrugged. 'Mind-reading was never one of my talents.'

His gaze hardened. 'Then let me give it to you in words of one syllable, just so there can be no misunderstanding.' There was a pause. 'Just stay away from my brother, okay?'

She stared at him in disbelief. 'Excuse me?'

'You heard. Leave him alone. Find someone else to dig your beautiful claws into—I'm sure there must be plenty of takers.'

His hand was still on her arm and to the outside world it must have looked like an affectionate gesture between two people who'd just bumped into one another, but to Keeley it felt nothing like that. She could feel the imprint of his fingers through her sweater and it was almost as if he were branding her with his touch—as if he were setting her skin on fire. Angrily, she shook herself free. 'I can't believe you have the nerve to come out and say something like that.'

'Why not? I have his best interests at heart.'

'You mean you regularly go around warning off Pavlos's friends?'

'Up until now I haven't felt the need to do more than keep a watchful eye on them but today I do. Funny that.' He gave a mirthless smile. 'I have no idea of your success rate with men, though I imagine it must be high.

But I feel I'd better crush any burgeoning hopes you may have by telling you that Pavlos already has a girlfriend. A beautiful, decent woman he cares for very much and wedding bells are in the air.' His eyes glittered. 'So I wouldn't bother wasting any more time on him if I were you.'

It struck Keeley again how *controlling* he was. Even now. As if all he had to do was to snap his fingers and everyone would just jump to attention. 'And does he have any say in the matter?' she demanded. 'Have you already chosen the engagement ring? Decided where the wedding is going to be and how many bridesmaids?'

'Just stay away from him, Keeley,' he snapped. 'Understand?'

The irony was that Keeley had absolutely no romantic leanings towards Pavlos Kavakos and never had done. They'd once been close, yes—but in a purely platonic way and she hadn't seen him in years. Their current friendship, if you could call it that, extended no further than her pressing the occasional 'like' button or smiley face whenever he posted a photo of himself with a crowd of beautiful young things revelling in the sunshine. Meeting him today had been comforting because she realised he didn't care what had happened in the past, but she was aware that they moved in completely different worlds which never collided. He was rich and she was not. She didn't know or care that he had a girlfriend, but hearing Ariston's imperious order was like a red rag to a bull.

'Nobody tells me what to do,' she said quietly. 'Not you. Not anyone. You can't move people around like pawns. I'll see who I want to see—and you can't do a thing to stop me. If Pavlos wants to get in touch, I'm not going to turn him away just because *you* say so. Understand?'

She saw the disbelief on his face which was quickly followed by anger, as if nobody ever dared defy him so openly, and she tried to ignore the sudden sense of foreboding which made her body grow even more tense. But she'd said her piece and now she needed to get away. Get away quickly before she started thinking about how it had felt to have him touch her.

She turned away and walked straight out of the gallery, not noticing that her cream shawl had slipped from her nerveless fingers. All she was aware of was the burn of Ariston's eyes on her back, which made each step feel like a slow walk to the gallows. The glass elevator arrived almost immediately but Keeley was shaking as it zoomed her down to ground level and her forehead was wet with sweat as she stepped out onto the busy London pavement.

CHAPTER TWO

THE JOURNEY BACK to her home in New Malden passed in a blur as Keeley kept remembering the way Ariston had spoken to her—with a contempt he'd made no attempt to disguise. But that hadn't stopped her breasts from tightening beneath his arrogant scrutiny, had it? Nor that stupid yearning from whispering over her skin every time she'd looked into the blue blaze of his eyes. And now she was going to have to start forgetting him all over again.

A sudden spring shower emptied itself on her head as she emerged from the train station. The April weather was notoriously unpredictable but she was ill-prepared for the rain and hadn't packed an umbrella. By the time she let herself into her tiny bedsit she was dripping wet and cold and her fingers were trembling as she shut the door. But instead of doing the sensible thing of stripping off her clothes and boiling the kettle to make tea, she sank into the nearest chair, not caring that her clothes were damp and getting all crumpled. She stared out of the window but the rods of rain spattering onto the rooftops barely registered. Suddenly she was no longer sitting shivering in a small and unremarkable corner of London. Her mind was playing tricks on her and all she could see was a wide silver beach with beautiful mountains rising up in the distance. A paradise of a place. Lasia.

Keeley swallowed, unprepared for the sudden rush of memory which made the past seem so vivid. She remembered her surprise at finding herself on Lasia—a private island owned by the powerful Kavakos family, with whom she'd had no connection. She'd been staying on nearby Andros with her mother who had spent the holiday complaining about her recent divorce from Keeley's father and washing her woes away with too many glasses of *retsina*.

But Ariston's own father had been one of those men who were dazzled by celebrity—even B-list celebrity—and when he'd heard that the actress and her teenage daughter were so close, had insisted they join him on his exclusive island home to continue their holiday. Keeley had been reluctant to gatecrash someone else's house party but her mother had been overjoyed at the free upgrade, her social antennae quivering in the presence of so many rich and powerful men. She had layered on extra layers of 'war paint' and crammed her body into a bikini which was much too brief for a woman her age.

But Keeley had wanted none of the party scene because it bored her. Despite her relatively tender years, she'd had her fill of the decadent parties her mother had dragged her to since she'd been old enough to walk. At eighteen, she just tried to stay in the background because that was where she felt safest. Over the years her

mother's sustained girlishness had contributed to her becoming an out and out tomboy, despite her very bother-
some and very feminine curves. She remembered being
overjoyed to meet the sporty Pavlos, with whom she'd
hit it off immediately. The Greek teenager had taught
her how to snorkel in the crystal bays and taken her
hiking in the blue-green mountains. Physical attraction
hadn't come into it because, like many children brought
up by a licentious parent, Keeley had been something
of a prude. She'd never felt a single whisper of desire
and the thought of sex had been mildly disgusting. She
and Pavlos had been like brother and sister—growing
brown as berries as they explored the island paradise
which had felt like their own miniature kingdom.

But then one morning his older brother Ariston had
arrived in a silvery-white boat, looking like some kind
of god at its helm, with his tousled black hair, tawny
skin and eyes which matched the colour of the dark sea.
Keeley remembered watching him from the beach, her
heart crashing in an unfamiliar way. She remembered
her mouth growing dry as he jumped onto the sand, the
fine silver grains spraying up around his bronzed calves
like Christmas glitter. Later, she'd been introduced to
him but had remained so self-conscious in his presence that she'd barely been able to look him in the eye.
Not so all the other women at the house party. She'd
cringed at the way her mother had flirted with him—
even asking him to rub suncream into her shoulders.
Keeley remembered his barely perceptible shudder as
he delegated the task to a female member of staff, and
her mother's pout when he did so.

And then had come the night of the party—the impressive party to which the Greek Defence Minister had been invited. Keeley remembered the febrile atmosphere and Ariston's disapproving face as people started getting more and more drunk. Remembered wondering where her mother had disappeared to—only to discover that she'd been caught making out with the minister's driver, her blonde head bobbing up and down on the back seat of the official car as she administered oral sex to a man half her age. Someone had even filmed them doing it. And that was when all hell had broken loose.

Keeley had fled down to the beach, too choked with shame to be able to face anyone, too scared to read the disgust in their expressions and wanting nothing but to be left alone. But Ariston had come after her and had found her crying. His words had been surprisingly soft. Almost gentle. He'd put his arms around her, and it had felt like heaven. Was it because her mother never showed physical affection and her father had been too old to pick her up when she was little which had caused Keeley to misconstrue what was happening, so she mistook comfort for something else? Was that why the desire which had been absent from her life now shot through her like a flame, making her behave in a way she'd never behaved before?

It had been so powerful, that feeling. Like a primitive hunger which *had* to be fed. Pressing her body against Ariston's, she'd risen up on tiptoe as her trembling mouth sought his. After a moment he had responded and that response had been everything she could have dreamed of. For a few minutes the feeling had intensified as his lips had pressed down urgently against hers. She'd felt his tongue nudging against her mouth and she'd opened her mouth in silent invitation. And then his fingers had been on her quivering breasts, impatiently fingering her nipples into peaking points before guiding her hand towards his trousers. There had been no shyness on her part, just a glorious realisation of the power of her own sexuality—and his. She remembered the ragged groan he'd made as she'd touched him there. The way she'd marvelled at the hard ridge pushing against his trousers as, greedily, she had run her fingertips over it. Passion had swamped shyness and she'd been so consumed by it that she suspected she would have let him do whatever he wanted, right there and then on the silvery sand—until suddenly he had thrust her away from him with a look on his shadowed face which she would remember as long as she lived.

'You little…*tramp*,' he'd said, his voice shaking with rage and disgust. 'Like mother, like daughter. Two filthy little tramps.'

She'd never realised until that moment how badly rejection could hurt. Just like she hadn't realised how someone could make you feel so *cheap*. She remembered the shame which flooded through her as she vowed never to put herself in that position again. She would never allow herself to be rejected again. But her own pain had been quickly superseded by what had happened when they'd returned to England and her mother's lifestyle had finally caught up with her—and in one way and another they'd been paying the price ever since.

She pushed the bitter memories away because her

hair was still damp and she had now started to shiver so Keeley forced herself to get up and to go into the cramped bathroom, where the miserable jet of tepid water trickling from the shower did little to warm her chilled skin. But the brisk rub of a rough towel helped and so did the big mug of tea she made herself afterwards. She'd just put on her uniform when there was a knock on the door and she frowned. Her social circle was tiny because of the hours she worked, but even so she didn't often invite people here. She didn't want people coming in and judging her. Wondering how the only daughter of a wealthy man and an actress whose face had graced cinema screens in a series of low-budget vampire movies should have ended up living in such drastically reduced circumstances.

A louder knock sounded and she pulled open the door, her curiosity dying on her lips when she saw who was standing there. Her heart pounded in her chest as she looked into the blaze of Ariston's eyes and she gripped the door handle, hard. His black hair was wet and plastered to his head and his coat was spattered with raindrops. She knew she should tell him to get lost before slamming the door shut in his face but the powerful impact of his presence made her hesitate just as the siren tug of her body betrayed her yet again. Because he was just so damned *gorgeous*…with his muscular physique and that classical Greek face with the tiny bump midway down his nose.

'What are you doing here?' she said coldly. 'Did you think of a few more insults you'd forgotten to ram home?'

His lips curved into an odd kind of smile. 'I think you left…this.'

She stared down at the cream shawl he was holding, her heart automatically contracting. It was an old wrap which had belonged to her mother—a soft, cashmere drift of a thing embroidered with tiny pink flowers and green leaves. These days it was faded and worn, but it reminded her of the woman her mother used to be and a lump rose in her throat as she lifted her gaze to his.

'How did you find out where I live?' she questioned gruffly.

'It wasn't difficult. You signed the visitors' book at the gallery, remember?'

'But you didn't have to bring it yourself. Couldn't you have asked one of your minions to do it?'

'I could. But there are some things I prefer not to delegate.' He met her eyes. 'And besides, I don't think we've quite finished our conversation, do you?'

She supposed they hadn't and that somehow there seemed to be a lot which had been left unsaid. And maybe it was better that way. Yet something was stopping her from closing the door on him. She told herself he had gone out of his way to bring her mum's shawl back to her and he *was* very wet. Did he sense her hesitation? Was that why he took a step forward?

'So aren't you going to ask me inside?' he persisted softly.

'Suit yourself,' she said carelessly, but her heart was thumping like a crazy thing as she walked back into the little bedsit and heard him shut the door to follow her. And when she turned round and saw him standing there—so powerful and masculine—her breasts grew hot and heavy with desire. Why him? she thought despairingly. Why should Ariston Kavakos be the only man who should make her feel so insanely *alive*? Her smile was tight. 'Though if you're going to try to justify your ridiculously controlling behaviour, I wouldn't bother.'

'And what's that supposed to mean?' he questioned silkily.

'It means that you turn up and suddenly send your brother away to sea—just to get him away from me. Isn't that a little desperate?'

His lips hardened. 'Like I told you. He already has a girlfriend. A young woman of Greek origin who has just qualified as a doctor and is light years away from someone like you. And if you must know, the business in the Gulf is both urgent and legitimate—you flatter yourself if you think I'd manufacture some kind of catastrophe just to remove him from your company. But I'm not going to lie. I can't deny I'm happy he's gone.'

She felt the sting of his words yet she could almost understand his concern—even though it was misplaced—because the contrast between her and Pavlos's girlfriend couldn't have been greater. She could imagine how Ariston must see it, in that simplistic and chauvinistic way of his. The qualified professional doctor versus someone with barely an exam to her name. If he'd gone about it differently—if he'd asked her nicely—then Keeley might have done what he wanted her to do. She might have given him her word that she'd never see Pavlos again—which was probably true in any case. But he wasn't asking, was he? He was *telling*. And it wasn't so much the contempt in his eyes which was making her angry—it was the total lack of respect. As if she meant nothing. As if her feelings counted for nothing. As if she was to spend the rest of her life paying for one youthful mistake. She tilted her chin upwards. 'If you think you can tell me what to do, then you're wrong,' she said. 'Very, very wrong.'

Ariston stiffened because her defiance was turning him on and that was the last thing he wanted. He'd come here ostensibly to return the shawl she'd left behind and yet part of him had *wanted* to see her again, even though he'd convinced himself he was only looking out for his brother's welfare. In the car he had briefly buried his nose in the soft cashmere and smelt Keeley's faint and flowery perfume. He'd wondered whether she had deliberately left it behind to get his brother to come running after her when he arrived back in England. Had that been her not so subtle plan? Did she sense a softness in his younger sibling and a susceptibility to her blonde sexiness which could override what seemed to be a perfect relationship with his long-term girlfriend?

He remembered how close she and Pavlos had been on that holiday, how they used to run around together all the time. People said the past had powerful and sentimental tentacles and she'd known his brother when he was young and impressionable. Long before he'd reached the age of twenty-five and come into the massive trust fund which had changed people's attitude towards him, because wealth always did. Mightn't Pavlos read more into his date with the sexy blonde than there really was and forget the safe and settled future which was carefully laid out for him? What if Keeley Turner realised that a fortune was there for the taking if she just went about it the right way?

He glanced around her home, more surprised by her environment than he could remember being surprised by anything in a long time. Because this wasn't just a low standard of living—this was *breadline* living. He'd imagined peacock feathers and glittery necklaces draped over mirrors. Walls dripping with old photos depicting her mother's rather tawdry fame, but there was nothing other than neatness and an almost bland utilitarianism. The most overriding feature was one of *cleanliness*. His mouth hardened. Was that simply a clever ploy to illustrate what a good little homemaker she could be, if only some big and powerful man would take her away from all this and give her the opportunity?

He'd been doing his best not to stare at her because staring only increased his desire and a man could think more clearly when his blood wasn't heated by lust. But now he looked at her dispassionately and for the first time he registered that she was wearing some kind of *uniform*. He frowned. Surely she wasn't a nurse? He took in a shapeless navy dress edged by a paler blue piping and then noticed a small badge depicting a bright, cartoon sun and what looked like a chicken drumstick underneath the words 'Super Save'. No. His mouth twisted. Definitely not a nurse.

'You work in a shop?' he demanded.

He could see the indecision which fretworked her

brow, before she gave him another defiant tilt of her chin which made her lips look utterly kissable.

'Yes, I work in a shop,' she said.

'Why?'

'Why not?' she questioned angrily. 'Somebody has to. How else do you think all the shelves get stacked with new produce? Or, let me guess—you never actually *do* your own shopping?'

'You're a shelf-stacker?' he asked incredulously.

Keeley drew in a deep breath. If it had been anyone else she might have blurted out the truth about her mother and all the other dark stuff which had led her to having to leave so many jobs that, in the end, Super Save supermarket had been her unlikely saviour. She might have explained that she was doing her best to make up for all those lost, gypsy-like years by studying hard whenever she had a spare moment and was doing an online course in bookkeeping and business studies. She might even have plunged the very depths of her own despair and conveyed the sense of hopelessness she felt when she visited her mother every week. When she saw how the once vibrant features had become an unmoving mask while those china-blue eyes stared unseeingly into the distance. When, no matter how many times she prayed for a different outcome, her mother failed to recognise the young woman she had given birth to.

Briefly Keeley closed her eyes as she remembered the awkward conversation she'd had last week with the care-home manager. How she'd been informed that costs were spiralling and they were going to have to put the fees up and that there was only so much that the welfare state could do. And when she'd tried to protest about her mum being moved to that horrible great cavern of a place which was not only cheaper but miles away, she had been met with a shrugging response and been told that nobody could argue with economics.

But why imagine that Ariston Kavakos would have anything other than a cold and unfeeling heart? As if he would even *care* about her problems. The controlling billionaire clearly wanted to think the worst about her and she doubted whether coming out with her own particular sob story would change his mind. Suddenly she felt sorry for Pavlos. How awful to have a brother who was so determined to orchestrate your life that you weren't allowed the personal freedom to make your own friends. Why, the sexy Greek billionaire standing in front of her was nothing more than a raging megalomaniac!

'Yes, I'm a shelf-stacker,' she said quietly. 'Do you have a problem with that?'

Ariston wanted to say that the only problem he had was with *her*. With her inherent sensuality, which managed to transcend even the ugly outfit she was wearing. Or maybe it was because he'd seen her in a swimsuit, with the sopping wet fabric clinging to every feminine curve. Maybe it was because he knew what a killer body lay beneath the oversized uniform which was making him aroused. Yet it was a shock to discover just how humble her circumstances were. As a gold-digger she clearly wasn't as effective as her mother had been or she wouldn't have ended up in a crummy apartment, working unsociable hours in a supermarket.

In his mind he began to do rapid calculations. She was obviously broke and therefore easy to manipulate, but he also sensed that she presented an unknown kind of danger. If it hadn't been for Pavlos he would have fought the infuriating desire to kiss her and just walked away, consigning her to history. He would have phoned the sizzling supermodel he'd taken to the photographic exhibition and demanded she drop everything. Especially her panties. He swallowed, because the equally infuriating reality was that the model seemed instantly forgettable when he compared her to Keeley Turner in her unflattering uniform. Was it the fire spitting from her green eyes and the indignant tremble of those lips which made him want to dominate and subdue her? Or because he wanted to protect his brother from someone like her? He'd sent Pavlos off to sea to deal with a crew in revolt—but as soon as the situation was resolved he would return. And who was to say what the two of them might get up to if his back was turned? He couldn't keep them apart—no matter how powerful he was. Mightn't her ethereal blonde beauty tempt his brother into straying, despite the lovely young woman waiting for him in Melbourne?

Suddenly his thoughts took on a completely different direction as a solution came out of nowhere. A solution of such satisfying simplicity that it almost took his breath away. Because weren't men territorial above all else—especially Kavakos men? He and Pavlos hadn't been brought up to share—not their toys, nor their thoughts, and certainly not their women. The age difference between them had guaranteed that just as much as the bleak and unsettled circumstances of their childhood. So what if *he* seduced her before his brother got a chance? Pavlos certainly wouldn't be interested in one of *his* cast-offs—so wouldn't that effectively remove her from his brother's life for good?

Ariston swallowed. And sex might succeed in eradicating her from *his* mind, once and for all. Because hadn't she been like a low-grade fever all these years—a fever which still flared up from time to time? She was the only woman he'd ever kissed and not had sex with and perhaps it was his need for perfection and completion which demanded he remedy that aching omission.

He looked around her shabby home. At the thin curtains at the window which looked out over a rainy street and the threadbare rug on the floor. And suddenly he realised it could be easy. It always was with women, when you brought up the subject of cash. His mouth hardened with bitter recall as he remembered the monetary transaction which had defined and condemned him when he had been nothing more than a boy. 'Do you need money?' he questioned softly. 'I rather think you do, *koukla mou.*'

'You're offering me money to stay away from your brother? Seriously?' She stared at him. 'Isn't that what's known as blackmail?'

'Actually, I'm offering you money to come and work for me. More money than you could have ever dreamed of.'

'You mean you have your own supermarket?' she questioned sarcastically. 'And need your very own shelf-stacker?'

He very nearly smiled but forced himself to clamp his lips together before returning her gaze. 'I haven't been tempted into retail as of yet,' he said drily. 'But I have my own island, on which I occasionally entertain. In fact, I'm flying back there tomorrow to prepare for a house party.'

'How nice for you. But I don't see what that has to do with me. Am I supposed to congratulate you on having so many friends—even though it's difficult to believe you actually have *any*?'

A pulse began to beat insistently at his temple because Ariston wasn't used to such a feisty and insolent reaction—and never from a woman. Yet it made him want to pull her into his arms and crush his lips down hard against hers. It made him want to push her up against the wall and have her moaning with pleasure as he slid his fingers inside her panties. He swallowed. 'I'm telling you because during busy times on the island, there is always work available for the right person.'

'And you think I'm the right person?'

'Well, let's not push credibility too far.' His lips twisted as he looked around. 'But you're clearly short of money.'

'I'm sure most people are compared to you.'

'We're talking about your circumstances, Keeley, not mine. And this apartment of yours is surprisingly *humble*.'

Keeley didn't deny it. How could she? 'And?'

'And I'm curious. How did that happen? How did you get from being flown around Europe on private jets to… this? Your mother must have made a stack of money from her various *liaisons* with wealthy men and her habit of giving tell-all interviews to the press. Doesn't she help fund her daughter's lifestyle?'

Keeley stared him out, thinking how very wrong he'd got it but she wasn't going to tell him. Why should she? Some things were just too painful to recount, especially to a cold and uncaring man like him. 'That's none of your business,' she snapped.

A calculating look entered his eyes. 'Well, whatever it is you're doing—it clearly isn't working. So how about earning yourself a bonus?' he continued softly. 'A big, fat bonus which could catapult you out of the poverty trap?'

She looked at him suspiciously, trying to dampen down the automatic spring of hope in her heart. 'Doing what?'

He shrugged. 'Your home is surprisingly clean and tidy, so I assume you're capable of doing housework. Just as I assume you're able to follow simple instructions and help around the kitchen.'

'And you trust me enough to employ me?'

'I don't know. Can I?' His gaze seared into her. 'I imagine the reason for your relative poverty is probably because you're unreliable and easily bored by the mundane—and that maybe things didn't fall into your lap as effortlessly as you thought they might. Am I right, Keeley? Did you discover that you weren't as successful a freeloader as your mother?'

'Go to hell,' she snapped.

'But I suspect that if the price was right you would be prepared to knuckle down,' he added thoughtfully.

'So how about if I offered you a month as a temporary domestic on my Greek estate—and the opportunity to earn yourself the kind of money which could transform your life?'

Her heart was beating very hard. 'And why would you do that?' she croaked.

'You know why.' His voice grew harsh. 'I don't want you in London when Pavlos returns. He's due to fly to Melbourne in two weeks' time, hopefully with a diamond ring tucked inside his pocket—and after that, I don't care what you do. Let's just call it an insurance policy, shall we? I'm prepared to pay a big premium to keep you out of my brother's life.'

His disapproval washed over her like dirty water and Keeley wanted to tell him exactly what he could do with his offer, yet she couldn't ignore the nagging voice in her head which was urging her to be realistic. Could she really afford to turn down the kind of opportunity which would probably never come her way again, just because she loathed the man who was making it?

'Tempted?' he questioned softly.

Oh, she was tempted, all right. Tempted to tell him that she'd never met anyone so charmless and insulting. Keeley felt her skin grow hot as she realised he was offering her a job as some kind of *skivvy*. Someone to get her hands dirty by tidying up after him and his fancy guests. To chop vegetables and change his bed while he cavorted on the silvery beach with whoever his current squeeze was—probably the stunning redhead he'd taken to the gallery opening with him. He was looking down his proud and patrician nose at her and she opened her mouth to say she'd rather starve than accept his offer until she reminded herself of the significant fact she'd been in danger of forgetting. Because it wasn't just herself she had to consider, was it?

She stared down at one of the holes in the carpet as she thought of her mother and the little treats which added to her life, even though she was completely oblivious to them. The weekly manicure and occasional hairdo to primp those thinning curls into some sort of shape, so that in some ways she resembled the woman she had once been. Vivienne Turner didn't *know* that these things were being done for her, but Keeley did. Sometimes she shuddered to imagine what her mother's reaction would have been if she'd been able to look into a crystal ball and see the life she'd been condemned to live. But nobody had a crystal ball, thank goodness. Nobody could see what lay ahead. And when occasionally other patients' relatives or members of staff recognised the shell of the woman who had once been Vivienne Turner, Keeley was proud that her mother looked as good as she possibly could. Because that would have mattered. To her.

So test him, she thought. See what the mighty Ariston Kavakos is putting on the table. See if it's big enough to enable you to endure his company for longer than a minute. 'How much,' she said baldly, 'are you offering me?'

Ariston swallowed down his distaste as he heard the shrewd note which had entered her voice and he realised that Keeley's greed was as transparent as her mother's. His mouth twisted. How he despised her and everything she stood for. Yet his natural revulsion was not enough to destroy his desire for her and his mouth grew dry as he thought about having sex with Keeley Turner. Because it was inconceivable that she would return to Lasia and *not* sleep with him. It would bring about satisfaction and closure—for both of them. The fever in his blood would be removed and afterwards she could be quietly airbrushed from all their lives. She would be rewarded with enough money to satisfy her. She would disappear into the sunset. Most important of all—Pavlos would never see her again.

He smiled as he mentioned a sum of money, expecting her simpering gratitude and instant acceptance, but instead he was met with a look from her green eyes which was almost glacial.

'Double it,' she said coolly.

Ariston's smile died but he could feel the insistent beat of lust intensifying because her attitude made his callous plan a whole lot easier to execute. Every woman could be bought, he remembered bitterly. You just had to negotiate the right price.

'You have a deal,' he said softly.

CHAPTER THREE

LASIA WAS AS beautiful as Keeley remembered it. No. Maybe even more so. Because when you were eighteen you thought that sunny days would never end and beauty would last for ever. You never imagined that life could turn out so different from how you'd imagined. She'd thought the money would last. She'd thought...

No. She gazed out of the car window at the cloudless blue sky. She wasn't going to do that thing. She wasn't going to *look back*. She was here, on this stunning private island, to work for Ariston Kavakos and earn herself a nest egg for her poor, broken mother. Fixing her gaze on the dark blue line of the horizon, she reminded herself to start looking for the positives, not the negatives.

A fancy car had been waiting for her on Lasia's only airstrip—its air-conditioned interior deliciously welcoming because, even though it was still only springtime, the midday sun was intense. During the flight over she'd wondered if any of Ariston's staff might remember her and she was dreading any such recognition. But thankfully the driver was new—well, new to her—and his name was Stelios.

He seemed content to remain silent and Keeley said nothing as the powerful car snaked its way through the mountain roads towards the Kavakos complex on the other side of the island. But although outwardly calm, inside she was quaking for all kinds of reasons. For a start, she'd lost her job at the supermarket. Her manager had reacted with incredulity when she'd asked for a month's unpaid holiday, telling her that she must have taken leave of her senses if she expected *those* kinds of perks. He'd added rather triumphantly that she was in the wrong job, but deep down Keeley had already known that. Because no matter how hard she'd tried, she'd never fitted in. Not there. Not anywhere if she stopped to think about it—and certainly not here, on this private paradise which exuded untold wealth and privilege. Where costly yachts bobbed on the azure sea as carelessly as a baby floated toys in the bathtub. She leaned forward to get a better look as the car rounded the bend and made its slow descent towards the complex she'd last seen when she was eighteen, blinking her eyes in surprise because everything looked so different.

Oh, not Assimenos Bay—that hadn't changed. The natural cove with its silvery sand was as stunning as ever, but the vast house which had once dominated it had gone. The beachside mansion was no more and in its place stood an imposing building which seemed composed mainly of glass. Modern and magnificent, the transparent walls and curved windows reflected back the different hues of sea and sky so that Keeley's first impression was that everything looked so *blue*. As blue as Ariston's eyes, she found herself thinking, before reminding herself furiously that she wasn't here to fantasise about him.

And then, as if she had conjured him up from her restless imagination, she saw the Greek tycoon standing at one of the vast windows on the first floor of the house. Standing watching her—his stance as unmoving as a statue. A ripple of unwilling awareness ran through her body as she stared up at him because even at a distance he dominated everything. Even though she was surrounded by so much natural beauty and the kind of scenery she hadn't seen in a long time it still took a huge effort to drag her gaze away from him. And she mustn't be seen ogling him like some helpless fan-girl. Hadn't she made that mistake once before? And look where that had got her. This was her chance to redeem herself and the only way she could achieve that was by remaining immune to him and his effortless charisma. To show him she no longer wanted him—that ship had sailed—because she wasn't into cruel billionaires who treated you with zero respect.

The car stopped and Stelios opened the door and Keeley could smell lemons and pine and the salty tang of the nearby sea as she stepped onto the sun-baked courtyard.

'Here's Demetra,' said Stelios as a middle-aged woman in a crisp white uniform began walking through the shimmering heat towards them. 'She's the cook—but basically she's in charge! Even Ariston listens when Demetra speaks. She'll show you to your accommodation. You're pretty lucky to be staying here,' he observed. 'All the other staff live in the village.'

'Thank you.' Keeley turned to him in surprise. 'You speak perfect English!'

'Pretty much. I lived in London for a while. Used to drive taxis for a living.' Stelios gave an inscrutable smile. 'Though the boss doesn't like me to publicise it too much.'

No, she'd bet he didn't. A silent but understanding driver would be an asset for a control freak like Ariston, thought Keeley wryly. Someone able to eavesdrop on the conversation of his English-speaking guests should the need arise. Yet she heard the obvious affection in the driver's voice as he referred to his boss and wondered what the autocratic ship-owner had ever done to deserve it, apart from be born with a silver spoon in his mouth. But everyone liked you when you had money, she reminded herself. The world was full of hangers-on who were mesmerised by the lure of wealth. The same hangers-on who would drop you like a hot potato when all that wealth had gone.

She smiled as the cook approached, reminding herself it was important to be accepted by the people she was going to be working with and to show them she wasn't afraid of hard work.

'*Kalispera*, Demetra,' she said, holding out her hand. 'I'm Keeley. Keeley Turner.'

'*Kalispera*,' said the cook, looking pleased. 'You speak Greek?'

'Not really. Only a couple of phrases.' Keeley pulled a face. 'But I'd love to learn more. Do you speak English?'

'*Neh*. Kyrios Kavakos likes all his staff to speak English.' She smiled. 'We help each other. Come. I show you your house.'

Keeley followed the cook down a narrow sandy path leading directly to the beach, until they reached a small whitewashed cottage. She could hear the waves lapping against the shore and could see the moving glimmer of sunlight on the water, but, although she was surrounded by so much beauty, all she could remember was the uproar and the chaos. Because wasn't it over there beside that crop of rocks that Ariston pulled her into his arms for that tantalisingly sweet taste of pleasure, before thrusting her away again? She closed her eyes as goosebumps shivered over her bare arms, despite the heat of the day. How could the memory of something which had happened so long ago still be so vivid?

'You like it?' questioned Demetra, obviously misinterpreting her silence.

'Oh, gosh, yes. It's…beautiful,' said Keeley quickly.

Demetra smiled. '*Oreos*. All Lasia is *oreos*. Come to the house when you are ready and I show you everything.'

After Demetra had gone, Keeley went inside the cottage—leaving the door open so she could hear the waves as she set about exploring her temporary home. It didn't take long to get her bearings because, although it was small and compact, it was still bigger than her home in London. There was a sitting room and a small kitchen, while upstairs was a bedroom with space for little more than a large bed. The bathroom was surprisingly sophisticated and the whole place was simple and clean, with walls painted white and completely bare of decoration. But the light which flooded into every room was incredible—bright and clear and shot with the dancing reflection of the waves. Who needed pictures on the walls when you had that?

Keeley unpacked, showered and changed into shorts and a T-shirt—and was just making her way downstairs when she saw Ariston walking towards her cottage. And try as she might, she could do nothing to prevent the powerful squeeze of her heart and the molten tug deep inside her.

She wanted to turn away. To close her eyes and shut him out…yet she wanted to watch him like the rerun of a favourite TV show. The powerful thrust of his thighs as he walked. The broadness of his shoulders and the bunched muscle of his arms. The way his white T-shirt contrasted with the darkness of his olive skin. Her mouth dried as she noticed the narrow band of skin showing above the low-slung waistband of his faded jeans. Because this was Ariston as she remembered him—not wearing a sophisticated suit which seemed to constrain him, but looking as if he could have just finished work on one of the fishing boats.

He was the most alpha male she'd ever seen but it was vital he didn't guess she thought that way. She was going to have to respond to him indifferently—betraying none of her uneasy emotions whenever he came close. She needed to pretend he was just like any other man—even though he wasn't. Because no other man had ever made her feel this way. She sucked in an unsteady breath as he approached, because the most important thing she needed to remember was that she didn't actually *like* him.

'So. Here you are,' he observed, his blue eyes moving over her with their strange, cold fire.

'Here I am.' Feeling curiously insubstantial, she tugged at the hem of her T-shirt. 'You sound surprised.'

'Maybe I am. Part of me wondered whether you might change your mind at the last minute and not bother coming.'

'Should I have done?' She fixed him with a questioning gaze. 'Would it have been wiser to have dismissed your generous job offer and carried on with my life the way it was, Kyrios Kavakos?'

As she stared at him so fearlessly, her bright green eyes so cat-like and entrancing, Ariston thought about the answers he *could* have given her. If she was someone he cared about he would have told her that, yes, she should have stayed well away from his island and the doomed orbit of a man like him. But the point was that he didn't care. She was a commodity. A woman he intended to seduce and finish what she had started all those years ago. Why warn her to be on her guard against something which was going to bring them both a great deal of pleasure?

And closure, he reminded himself grimly. Because wasn't closure equally important?

He stared at the thick pale hair which hung in a twisted rope over one shoulder, wondering why he found it so difficult to tear his eyes away from her. He'd known women more beautiful. He'd certainly known women more *suitable* than some washed-up ex-party-girl with dollar signs in her eyes. Yet knowing that did nothing to diminish her impact on him. Her lush breasts were pushing against a T-shirt the colour of the lemons which grew in the hills behind the house and a pair of cotton shorts skimmed her shapely hips and legs. She'd slipped her bare feet into a pair of sparkly flip-flops so that she looked unexpectedly carefree—and young—as if she hadn't made the slightest effort to impress him with her appearance and the unexpectedness of this made desire spiral up inside him even more.

'No, I think you're in exactly the right place,' he said evenly. 'So let's go into the house and I'll show you around. I think you'll find things have changed quite a lot since last time you were here.'

'No, honestly. You don't have to do that,' she said. 'Demetra has already offered.'

'But I'm offering now.'

She tilted her head to one side. 'Surely it would be more appropriate if another member of staff took me round? You must have plenty of other things you'd rather be doing—a busy man like you, with a great empire to control.'

'I don't care whether or not it's *appropriate*, Keeley. I happen to be a very hands-on employer.'

'And what you say goes, right?'

'Exactly. So why don't you just accept that, and do what I say?'

He was so ridiculously *masterful*, Keeley thought resentfully. Didn't he realise how out of touch and *outdated* he sounded when he spoke like that? But even though she objected to his overbearing attitude, she couldn't deny its effect on her. It was as if her body had been programmed to respond to his masculine dominance and there was nothing she could do to stop it. Her face was hot as she shut the cottage door and followed him across the beach towards his home, her flip-flops sinking into the soft sand as she scurried to match his pace.

'Any questions you want to ask?' he said, glancing down at her.

There were a million. She wanted to know why—at thirty-five and surely one of the world's most eligible bachelors—he still wasn't married. She wanted to know what made him so hard and cold and proud. She wanted to know if he ever laughed and if so, what made those sensual lips curve with humour. But she bit all those questions back because she had no right to ask them. 'Yes,' she said. 'What made you knock the old house down?'

Ariston felt a pulse flicker at his temple as he lessened his stride so she could keep up with him. How ironic that she should choose a subject which still had the power to make him feel uncomfortable. He remembered the disbelief he'd faced when he'd proposed demolition of the old house, which had been rich in history. How people had thought he was acting out of a sense of misplaced grief after the death of his father. But it had been nothing to do with that. For him it had been a necessary rebirth. Should he tell her that he'd wanted to raze away the past along with those impressive walls? As if believing that those dark memories could be reduced to rubble, just like the bricks. That he'd wanted to forget the house where his mother had played with him until the day she'd walked away—leaving him and Pavlos in the care of their father. Just as he wanted to forget the parties and sickly-sweet stench of marijuana and the women flown in from destinations all over Europe—their given brief to 'entertain' his father and his jaded friends. Why would he tell Keeley Turner something like that—when she and her mother had been exactly those kind of women?

'New broom, new era,' he said, with a hard smile. 'When my father died I decided I needed to make a few changes. To put my own stamp on the place.'

She was staring up at the wide glass structure. 'Well, you've certainly done that.'

Her cooing words sounded speculative—the instinctive reaction of an avaricious woman confronted by affluence—but that didn't quite cancel out the pleasure Ariston got from her praise. Or stop him thinking how much he'd like to hear that soft English voice whispering some very different things in his ear. Was she one of those women who talked during sex? he wondered. Or did she keep quiet until she started to come, gasping out her joyful pleasure into the man's ear? His lips curved into a speculative smile. He couldn't wait to find out.

He gestured for her to precede him though her wiggling bottom made it difficult for him to concentrate on the tour. He showed her the tennis court, the gym, his office and two of the smaller reception rooms—but decided against taking her upstairs to each of the seven en-suite bedrooms or, indeed, his own master suite. His throat tightened. Demetra could do that later.

At last he led her into the main sitting room, which was the focal point of the house, carefully watching her reaction as she was confronted by the sea view which dominated three of the massive glass walls. For a moment she stood there motionless—not appearing to notice the priceless Fabergé eggs which lay on one of the low tables, nor the rare Lysippos statue which he'd bought from under the noses of international dealers in an auction house in New York and which had sealed his reputation as a connoisseur of fine art.

'Wow,' she said indistinctly. 'Who came up with this?'

'I asked the architect to design me something to maximise the views and for each room to flow into the next,' he said. 'I wanted light and space everywhere—so that when I'm working it doesn't seem like being in the office.'

'I can't imagine any office looking like this. It looks...well, it's the most stunning place I've ever seen.' She turned to face him. 'The family business must be doing well.'

'Reassuringly well,' he said blandly.

'You're still building ships?'

He raised his eyebrows. 'My brother didn't tell you?'

'No, Ariston. He didn't tell me. We barely had time to reacquaint ourselves before you dragged him away.'

'Yes, we're still building ships,' he affirmed. 'But we're also making wines and olive oil on the other side of the island, which have become a surprising hit in all kinds of places. These days people seem to value organic goods and Kavakos products are on the shopping list of most of the world's big chefs.' He raised his eyebrows. 'Anything else you want to know?'

She brushed the palms of her hands down over her shorts. 'In England you said you were expecting guests this weekend.'

'That's right. Two of my lawyers are flying in from Athens for lunch tomorrow and there are five people arriving at the weekend for a house party.'

'And are they Greek?'

'International,' he drawled. 'You want to know who they are?'

'Isn't it always polite to know people's names in advance?'

'And handy when you're trying to research how much each is worth?' he offered drily. 'There's Santino Di Piero, the Italian property tycoon who is coming with his English girlfriend, Rachel. There's also a friend of mine from way back—Xenon Diakos who for some reason has decided to bring his secretary. I think her name is Megan.'

'That's four,' she said, determined not to rise to the nasty digs he was making.

'So it is. And Bailey Saunders is the other guest,' he said, as if he'd only just remembered.

'Her name seems familiar.' She hesitated. 'She's the woman you took to the opening night of the photographic exhibition, isn't she?'

'Is that relevant, Keeley?' he questioned silkily. 'Or, indeed, any of your business?'

She shook her head, not knowing why she'd mentioned it, and now she felt stupid—and vulnerable.

Embarrassed by her own curiosity and angry at the unwanted jealousy which was making her skin grow heated, Keeley walked over to the window and stared out unseeingly. Was she going to have to spend days witnessing Ariston making out with a beautiful woman? See them frolicking together in that amazing infinity pool or kissing on the beach in the moonlight? Would she have to change their bedsheets in the morning and see for herself the evidence of their shared passion? A shiver of revulsion shot through her and she prayed it didn't show. Because even if she had to contend with those things—so what? Ariston was nothing to her and she was nothing to him and unless she remembered that, she was going to have a very difficult month ahead of her.

'Of course it's none of my business,' she said stiffly. 'I didn't mean to—'

'Didn't mean to what?' He had walked across the room to stand beside her at the window and she found herself inhaling his subtle citrusy scent. 'Check out whether or not I had a girlfriend? Find out whether or not I was available? Don't worry, Keeley—I'm used to women doing that.'

She struggled to say something conventional. To make some witty remark which might dissolve the sudden tension which had suddenly sprung up between them. To act as if she didn't care or take him to task for his spectacular arrogance. But he was standing so close that she couldn't think of a single word, and even if she could she didn't think she'd be capable of saying it with any degree of conviction. Just like she didn't seem capable of preventing the way he was making her feel—as if her body were no longer her own. As if it was silently responding to things she'd only ever dreamed of.

She looked up into his face to discover that his eyes had become smoky and it was as if he'd read her thoughts because suddenly he lifted his hand to frame her face with his fingers, and he smiled. It wasn't a particularly nice smile and it didn't even reach his eyes but the sensation of his touch sent Keeley's already heightened senses into overdrive. His thumb stroked its way over her bottom lip so that it began to tremble uncontrollably. That was the only thing he was doing and yet it was making her want to melt. He was making her more aroused by the second and surely that must show. Her nipples had hardened into two painful little points and somewhere low in her belly she could feel a distracting and molten ache.

Did he realise that? Was that why his hold on her changed so that instead of cupping her face with his fingers, he was pulling her towards him? Pulling her into his arms as if it were his right to do so. His eyes were blazing as they stared into hers and she could feel the softness of her body moulding perfectly into the hardness of his, as he brought his mouth down on hers.

And Keeley shuddered because this was like no other kiss. It was like every fantasy she'd ever had— and wasn't the truth of it that those fantasies had always involved *him*? He kissed her slow and then he kissed her hard. He kissed her until she was squirming, until she thought she would cry out with pleasure. She could feel the rush of heat and the clamour of frustration and all she wanted was to give into that feeling. To wrap her arms around his neck and let desire take over. Whisper in his ear to have him do whatever he wanted. What she wanted. Have him ease this terrible ache inside her as she suspected only he could.

And then what? Let him take you to his bed even though you know how much he despises you? Even though Bailey Saunders is arriving in a couple of days? Because that was how these people operated. She'd seen for herself the world in which he lived. Easy come, easy go.

It didn't mean anything. *She* didn't mean anything—hadn't he already made that abundantly clear? And for someone with an already shaky sense of self-worth, such an action would be completely insane.

'No!' Keeley jerked away from him, taking a couple of steps back and trying to ignore the silent protest of her body. 'What the *hell* do you think you're doing, Ariston?' she demanded. 'Jumping on me like that!'

His short laugh was tinged with frustration. 'Oh, please,' he drawled. 'Please don't insult my intelligence, *koukla mou*—or your own for that matter. You were—*are*—hot and horny. You wanted me to kiss you and I was more than happy to oblige.'

'I did *not*,' she snapped back.

'Oh, Keeley—why deny the truth? Not the best start, in the circumstances—not when I consider honesty an invaluable asset for all my employees.'

'And surely crossing physical boundaries with your staff is unacceptable behaviour for any employer—have you stopped to consider *that*?'

'Maybe if you stopped looking at me with such blatant invitation,' he said silkily, 'then I might be able to stop responding to you as a man, rather than as a boss.'

'I was not!' she said indignantly.

'Weren't you? Ask yourself that question again, only this time don't lie to yourself.'

Keeley bit her lip. *Had* she been looking at him in invitation? Her heart pounded. Of course she had. And if she was being brutally honest, hadn't she wanted him to kiss her since she'd seen him standing at the windows of his glass mansion, his powerful physique dominating everything around him? Maybe even before that—when he'd come striding across the London gallery towards her and Pavlos with a face like thunder and a body which was tensed and powerful. And she mustn't let herself feel that way. She was here to earn money to help care for her stricken mother—not tangle with a self-confessed chauvinist like Ariston and get her heart broken in the process.

Drawing in a deep breath, she willed herself to at least *look* as if she were in control of her own emotions. 'I can't deny that there's an attraction between us,' she said. 'But that doesn't mean we're going to act on it. Not just because you're my boss and it's inappropriate, but because we don't even like each other.'

'What does liking have to do with it?'

'Are you serious?'

'Totally serious.' He shrugged. 'In my experience, a little hostility always adds a touch of spice. Surely your mama taught you that, Keeley?'

The implied slur piled on yet another layer of hurt

and Keeley wanted to hurl herself at him. To slam her fists angrily against that powerful chest and tell him to keep his opinions to himself because he didn't know what he was talking about. But she didn't trust herself to go near him because to touch him was to want him and she couldn't afford to put herself in that position again. He had asked for honesty, hadn't he? So why not just give it to him, even if it meant swallowing her pride in the process? Why pretend there was no elephant in the room when a whole herd of them were threatening to trample over her?

'I have no intention of getting close to you, Ariston, mainly because you're not the kind of man I like,' she said slowly. 'I came here to earn good money and that's what I intend to do. Actually, it's *all* I intend to do. I am going to work hard and to stay away from you as much as possible. I don't intend putting myself in a position of vulnerability again.' She forced a smile, injecting the requisite note of subservience into her voice, reminding herself to behave like the humble employee she was supposed to be. 'So if you'll excuse me—I'd better go and find out if there's anything Demetra wants me to do in the kitchen.'

CHAPTER FOUR

SHE WAS DRIVING him crazy.

Crazy.

Sucking in a lungful of air, Ariston dived beneath the inky waters of a sea just starting to be gilded by the sun coming up over the horizon. It was early. Too early for anyone else to be around. Not even the staff were awake yet and the shutters remained tightly closed in the bedroom windows of Keeley's cottage. And that was a pretty accurate metaphor for the current state of affairs between them, he thought grimly. For a man so utterly confident about his sexual power over women—and with good reason—things with Keeley Turner hadn't quite gone according to plan.

For a while he swam strongly beneath the shadowed surface of the water, trying to rid his body of some of the restless energy which had been building up inside him, but that was easier said than done. He had been sleeping badly, with images of Keeley in various imagined stages of undress haunting his erotic and frustrating dreams. Because she'd meant what she'd said, he was discovering with growing incredulity—and despite the sexual chemistry which sizzled so powerfully between them, she had stubbornly kept him at arm's length. He'd thought at first that her behaviour had been part of some contrived act intended to keep him on his toes. But there had been no relaxing of her attitude towards him. No sudden softening which might have indicated she was weakening. All interaction between them had followed a formal yet highly unsatisfactory path.

She politely enquired whether he would like coffee or bread, or water. She kept her eyes demurely lowered whenever their paths crossed. And no matter how many times he told her it was perfectly acceptable for her to use his Christian name in public, it fell on deaf ears. She was a conundrum, he thought. Was she really immune to the admiring glances she had attracted from his Athens-based lawyers when they had arrived on Lasia for lunch—or was she simply a very clever actress who knew the power of her own beauty? She acted as if she were made of marble, when he knew for a fact that beneath that cool and curvy exterior beat the heart of a passionate woman.

Had he thought that she would have succumbed to him by now? That the memory of the kiss they'd shared on her first day would have her sneaking in his arms to finish off what they'd started?

Of course he had.

That brief kiss had been the most erotic thing to happen to him in a long time but it had led precisely nowhere and although he wasn't a man used to being denied what he really wanted—he was now being forced to experience exactly that. So he'd been a little *distant* with her, intending to indicate his disapproval of women who teased, thinking his impatience would make her realise his patience was wearing thin. He'd anticipated her finding him alone in some quiet moment. He'd imagined her sliding down the zipper of his trousers and touching him where he ached to be touched. He swallowed. Any other woman would have done—and Keeley certainly had history on that score. If things had gone according to plan, by now he should have bedded her and enjoyed several sessions of mind-blowing sex. In fact, by now he probably would have been growing bored with her inevitable adoration and his only dilemma would be working out the best way to tell her it was over.

But it hadn't turned out like that.

She had thrown herself into her work with an enthusiasm which had taken him by surprise. Had she stacked supermarket shelves with such passion? he wondered wryly. Demetra had informed him that the Englishwoman was a joy to have around the kitchen and around the house. A joy? he wondered grimly. He had seen little evidence of it so far.

Was her frosty attitude intended to stoke up his sexual appetite? Because if that was the case then it was working. His blood pressure soared every time she walked onto the terrace in her crisp white uniform. The white cotton dress gave her a look of purity and her blonde hair was scraped neatly back into a no-nonsense chignon, which made her appear the perfect servant. Yet the glitter of fire in her green eyes whenever she was forced to meet his gaze was unmistakable—as if she was daring him to come near her again.

He resurfaced into the bright, golden morning, shaking droplets of water from his head before beginning to swim powerfully towards the shore. It was time to face the day ahead and to play at being host. Four of his guests had arrived but Bailey Saunders was no longer on the guest list. He'd phoned her a couple of days ago and asked for a rain check, and she had agreed. Of course she had. Women always did. He felt a beat of anticipation as he walked across the sand.

Maybe it was time for Keeley Turner to realise that it was pointless resisting the inevitable.

'Will you take the coffee out, Keeley?' Demetra pointed to the loaded tray.

'Of course.' Keeley smoothed down her white uniform dress. 'Shall I put some of those little lemon biscuits on a plate?'

'Efharisto.'

'Parakalo.' Automatically checking that she had everything she needed, Keeley carried it out onto the terrace with a heavy heart. Another trip to the table which had been set up next to the infinity pool, where Ariston was finishing a long lunch with his glamorous guests, and she was dreading it. Dreading seeing his rugged face watching her, his expression hidden behind his dark glasses as she tried to walk along the edge of the pool without appearing too self-conscious, but it was difficult. Just as it was difficult to forget that kiss they'd shared, when he'd made her usually non-responsive body spring to life—and left her in a state of frustrated arousal ever since. It was as if he'd lit the touchpaper of her repressed sexuality and set it on fire.

And she had only herself to blame.

Why hadn't she stopped him from pulling her into his arms like that? Because she'd been powerless to stop him. She had wanted him to do it. She still wanted him to do it.

She bit her lip. She'd done her best to push him to the back of her mind—avoiding him whenever possible and concentrating on her work, determined to do a job she could be proud of. She wanted to wipe out his negative impressions of her and show him she could be honest and hard-working and *decent*. Just like she was determined not to raise the suspicions of the people she worked with. She *liked* Demetra and Stelios, just as she liked the extra staff who'd been drafted in from the nearby village to help with the house party. She didn't want them to think she had some kind of *thing* with the boss. All she wanted was to be seen as the helpful Englishwoman who was eager to take on her fair share.

The sun was warm on her head as she took the coffee outside to where the five of them were sitting around the remains of the meal she'd served them—Xenon, Megan, Santino, Rachel and Ariston. She'd been introduced to them yesterday and they all seemed the jet-setting type of people she no longer associated with. She'd forgotten that life where women changed their outfits four times a day and spent more on a straw hat than Keeley spent on her entire summer wardrobe. She'd been as polite and as friendly as her position required but she was also aware that as a member of staff she was mostly invisible. Only the friendly Rachel had treated her as if she was a real person—and always made a point of chatting whenever she saw her.

Rachel's long, bronzed legs were stretched out in front of her and she brightened when she saw Keeley approaching with the silver coffee pot glinting in the sunshine.

'Oh, yum. I love this Greek coffee!' she said. 'It's so thick and sweet.'

'I won't make the obvious comparison,' commented Santino drily, easily catching the hastily balled napkin which his girlfriend hurled at him in mock rage.

Rachel took a small cup from the tray. 'Thanks, Keeley. Is it possible to have some more sparkling water? It's so hot today. You must be baking in that uniform,' she observed, with a frown. 'Does Ariston allow you to cool off in the pool or does he constantly keep your nose to the grindstone?'

'Oh, Keeley knows she has the run of the place when she isn't working,' murmured Ariston. 'She just chooses not to take advantage of it, don't you, Keeley?'

They were all looking at her and Keeley was acutely aware of the fact that Rachel and Megan were both wearing gauzy kaftans over tiny bikinis, while she was wearing a uniform which made her feel completely overdressed as well as overheated. All Ariston's staff wore uniforms—but somehow on her it looked all wrong. It was the right size and everything but it did unwanted things to her figure. It was the one thing she'd inherited from her mother which she could do nothing about. Because no matter how much she tried to disguise her shape with loose-fitting clothes, her bust always seemed too big and the curve of her hips that fraction too wide, so everything clung precisely where she didn't want it to cling.

'I have a great big ocean on my doorstep if ever I feel the need to swim, but when I'm not working I mostly spend time doing stuff on my computer,' she said and then, because they were still looking at her questioningly, she felt obliged to offer some kind of explanation. 'I'm studying for a diploma in business studies,' she added.

'Well, that's all very admirable but you need to take time off occasionally. What's it they say about all work and no play?' questioned Rachel, raking her fingers back through her dark hair and shooting Ariston a quizzical glance. 'Didn't you say that Bailey has bailed this weekend, if you'll excuse the pun?'

'Bailey is no longer coming, no,' Ariston said smoothly.

'So we'll be a woman short at dinner?' persisted Rachel.

'Oh, I'm sure you'll be able to cope with that,' said Santino. 'Since when did you ever worry about odd numbers, *cara*? You always seem to have enough conversation to compensate for any absent guests.'

'That much is true.' Rachel smiled. 'But why doesn't Keeley join us instead, to make the numbers up?'

Ariston removed his dark glasses and glimmered Keeley an unfathomable look. 'Yes,' he said, his velvety accent seeming to whisper like velvet across her skin. 'Why don't you join us for dinner later?'

She shook her head. 'No, honestly. I can't.'

'Why not? I'm giving you permission to take the evening off. In fact, look on it as an order.' His smile was hard and determined. 'I'm sure we have enough staff for you not to be missed waiting at table.'

'It's very…kind of you, but…' Keeley put the last of the coffee cups down with trembling fingers before straightening up. 'I don't have anything suitable to wear.'

It was the wrong thing to say. Why hadn't she just come out with an emphatic *no*?

'No worries. You're about the same size and height as me,' said Megan, looking her up and down. 'You can borrow something from me. Say yes, Keeley. You've been working so hard that you deserve a little downtime. And it would be my pleasure to lend you something.'

The two female guests were clearly on a mission to get her to change her mind and inwardly Keeley began to fume. She knew they were just trying to be kind, but she didn't want their kindness. It made her feel patronised but, even worse, it made her feel vulnerable. They thought they were giving her a treat but in reality they were pushing her closer to Ariston and that was a place she didn't want to be. But she could hardly give them the reason for her resistance, could she? She couldn't really tell them she was worried she would end up in bed with her boss! And in the end, opposition was pointless because it was five against one and there was no way she could get out of it.

You're having dinner with them, that's all, she reminded herself as she stood beneath the cool jets of the shower later that afternoon. All she had to do was put on a borrowed dress and try to be pleasant. She could leave whenever she wanted. *She didn't have to do anything she didn't want to do.*

Which was how she found herself walking towards the starlit terrace that evening, wearing the only dress of Megan's which fitted her and which was the last type of outfit she would normally have worn. It was too delicate. Too feminine. Too...*revealing.* In soft, blush pink, the low-cut bodice showcased her breasts and the silky fabric clung to her hips in precisely the way she didn't want it to. And she wasn't blind. Or stupid. She saw the way Ariston looked at her when she walked out onto the candlelit terrace. Saw the instinctive narrowing of his eyes, which set off an answering tightening in her breasts.

Her throat was so dry that she knocked back half a glass of champagne too quickly and it went straight to her head. It soothed her frazzled nerves but it also had the unwanted side effect of softening her reaction to her Greek boss, because naturally she found herself seated next to him. She told herself she wasn't going to be affected by him. That he was a callous manipulator who had no regard for her feelings. But somehow her thoughts weren't making it to her body. Her body didn't seem to be behaving itself at all.

She could feel it in the heavy rush of blood to her breasts and in her restlessness whenever Ariston subjected her to that cool stare, which he seemed to do far more than was necessary. And if that weren't bad

enough, she was having difficulty adjusting to this unexpected social outing. She hadn't been to a dinner
party this fancy for a long time and she'd never really
done so on her own terms before. She'd only ever been
invited because of her mother, and this was different.
She was no longer watching out of the corner of her eye
in case her mum did something outrageous, anxiously
wondering if she could get her home without making a
fool of herself. This time people seemed to be interested
in *her* and she didn't want them to be. What could she
say about herself—other than that she'd done a series
of menial jobs, because they were the only ones she
could get after a fractured education which had led to
zero qualifications?

She spent the evening blocking questions—something she'd learnt to do over the years—so that whenever she was asked something personal, she turned it
around and moved the subject swiftly onto something
else. She had become highly accomplished in the art
of evasion but tonight it seemed to be having entirely
the wrong effect. Was her elusiveness the reason why
Santino began to monopolise her for the second part
of the evening, while Rachel's pinched face seemed to
indicate she was regretting her impetuous decision to
have her join them? Keeley felt like standing up and an-
nouncing that she wasn't remotely interested in the Italian businessman—that there was only one man around
the table who had her attention and she was having to
fight very hard not to be mesmerised by him. Because
tonight Ariston looked amazing—very traditional and
heart-stoppingly masculine. His white shirt was unbut-

toned at the neck revealing a silky triangle of olive skin, and his tapered dark trousers emphasised his long legs and the powerful shafts of his thighs.

And all the while he was watching her, his blue gaze burning into her so intently that the breath caught in her throat and she was barely able to eat. Course after course of delicious food was placed in front of her, but Keeley could do little more than push it around her plate. Were the other guests amused by her lack of appetite—not realising the cause of it—especially as she seemed almost to be bursting out of Megan's dress? Did they think she was one of those women who never ate in public but enjoyed secret binges with the biscuit packet whenever she was alone?

'Enjoying yourself, Keeley?' asked Ariston softly.

'Very much,' she said, not caring if he heard the lie in her voice. Because what else could she say? That she could feel ripples of awareness whispering over her skin whenever he looked at her? That she found his hard and rugged profile the most beautiful thing she'd ever seen and she wanted nothing more than to just sit and stare at it?

She broke the mould of her Cinderella evening by excusing herself long before midnight. As soon as the clock struck eleven she stood up and politely thanked them for a lovely dinner. Somehow she maintained her high-headed posture as she walked away from the terrace but as soon as she was out of sight, she began to run. Along the path leading to the beach she ran, straight past her cottage and down to the shoreline, glad she was wearing her practical sandals underneath the long dress. And glad too that the waves were pounding against the sand so that the heavy sound drummed out the beating of her thudding heart. Picking up the hem of her dress, she stood back, careful not to let the sea-water touch the delicate fabric as she stared out at the moon-dappled water.

She remembered how she'd felt when the supermarket had sacked her just before she'd flown to Lasia, when she'd been swamped by the sense of having no real place in the world. She could feel it now—because she hadn't really been part of that glamorous table, had she? She'd been the outsider who had been dressed up for the occasion in a stranger's dress. Had Ariston known how alienated she'd felt—or was he too busy reeling her in with his potent sexuality to care? Didn't he realise that what was probably just a game to him meant so much more to someone like her who didn't have his tight circle of friends, or wealth, to fall back on?

She felt stupid tears stinging her eyes and wondered if they had been caused by self-pity. Because if they were she was going to have to lose them—and quickly. Count your blessings, she told herself fiercely as she rubbed her eyes with the back of her hand. Just be glad you've been strong enough to resist someone who could never be anything more than a one-night stand.

But as she turned to walk back towards her cottage she saw a figure walking towards her—a man she recognised in a heartbeat, even from this distance. How could she fail to recognise him when his image was burned so powerfully onto her mind that she could picture him at the slightest provocation? His shadowy figure was powerful as he moved and the glint of moonlight in his eyes and the paleness of his silk shirt captured her imagination. She felt her skin prickle with instinctive excitement, which was quickly followed by a cold wash of dismay as he approached, because she'd tried to do the right thing. She'd done everything in her power to stay away from him. *So why the hell was he here?*

'Ariston,' she said steadily. 'What are you doing here?'

'I was worried about you. You left dinner so abruptly and I watched as you took the path to your cottage.' His eyes narrowed as they swept over her. 'Only no light came on.'

'You were spying on me?'

'Not really. I'm your employer.' His voice sounded deep above the soft lapping of the waves. 'I was merely concerned for your welfare.'

Her eyes met his. 'Is that so?'

There was a pause. 'Yes. No,' he negated and suddenly his voice had grown harsh. 'Actually, I don't know. I don't know what the hell it is. All I know is that I can't seem to stop thinking about you.'

Keeley saw the sudden change in him. The tension which stiffened his body, which she suspected mirrored the tension in her own. Just as she knew what was about to happen from the look on his face—a raw look of hunger which set off an answering need somewhere deep inside her.

'Ariston,' she whispered, but it sounded more like a prayer than a protest as he pulled her into his arms, into the warmth of his embrace, and she let him—ignoring the objections which were crowding her mind. And the moment he touched her, she was lost.

He drove his mouth down on hers and she heard his little moan of triumph as she kissed him back. Her lips opened and he slid his tongue inside her mouth to deepen the kiss. She swayed against him, her finger-nails digging into his chest through the fine silk of his shirt, and he circled his hips against hers in a move-ment which was unashamedly urgent. And now his hand was slipping inside the bodice of her dress so he could cup her braless breast with his fingers and she let him do that, too. How could she stop him when she wanted it so much?

His groan was muffled as he explored each diamond-tipped nipple and she could feel her panties growing moist. Was he going to do it to her now? Here? Push her down onto the soft sand without giving her time to object? Yes. She would welcome that. She didn't want anything to destroy the mood or the moment, because this had been a long time coming. Eight years, to be precise. Eight long and arid years when her body had felt as if it were made of cardboard, rather than respon-sive flesh and blood. Keeley swallowed. She didn't want time to have second thoughts about what was about to happen—she wanted to just go with the flow and be spontaneous. A rush of excitement flooded through her until she remembered what she was wearing and, un-locking her lips from his, she pulled away from him. 'The dress!' she stumbled.

He stared down at her uncomprehendingly. 'The dress?' he echoed dazedly.

'It's not mine, remember? I don't want to…to mark it.'

'Of course. You borrowed the dress.' Something hardened in his eyes as his gaze swept over her and his smile was tinged with a flicker of triumph as he picked her up and walked across the sand towards the cottage, before kicking open the door.

CHAPTER FIVE

ONCE INSIDE, ARISTON carried Keeley straight upstairs in a display of masculine dominance she found intoxicating. As he brushed hungry kisses over her neck and lips she was on such a delirious high of pleasure that she was barely aware of him lifting her arms above her head and peeling off her borrowed dress. Until suddenly she was standing in front of him wearing nothing but a pair of tiny thong panties. Half naked in the silver moonlight, she should have felt shy, but the look blazing from Ariston's eyes made her feel anything *but* shy. Tilting her chin, she felt the silky movement of her hair as it swayed against her bare back and a sudden sense of liberation rippled through her as she met his slow and appreciative smile.

'*Theos mou*, but you are magnificent,' he said, his body tensing as he cupped one of her breasts like a market trader calculating the weight of a watermelon.

And even that rather brutal gesture excited her. Every single thing about him was exciting right now—each nerve ending in her body feeling as if a layer of skin had been peeled away, leaving her raw and aching. His voice dipped approvingly as his gaze focussed on her tiny panties. 'It seems that beneath the often unexceptional clothes you favour, you dress in order to please your man.' He glittered her a smile. 'And I approve.'

His arrogance was breathtaking and Keeley wanted to tell him that his words were inaccurate on so many counts. That the tiny briefs were the only thing she *could* have worn under such a flimsy gown without getting a visible panty line and usually she wore a heavy-duty bra to contain her overripe breasts. But he was playing with her nipples again and it was such an unbearably sweet sensation that she didn't have the desire—or the strength—to break the fragile mood with stumbled words of explanation. Because during that short journey from beach to bedroom she'd known there was to be no turning back. It didn't seem to matter if it was right or wrong, it just seemed inevitable. She was going to let Ariston Kavakos make love to her tonight and nothing was going to stop her.

She lifted her gaze to his, watching as he began to unbutton his shirt, his eyes not leaving her face as he bared his hair-roughened chest.

'Play with your breasts,' he ordered softly. 'Touch yourself.'

The words should have shocked her but they didn't—maybe because he'd managed to turn them into an irresistible and silky command. Should she tell him that her sexual experience was laughably lacking and she wasn't sure how good she would be? But if she was going to do this, she needed to do it without any hang-ups. Tentatively, she spread her palms over the aching mounds and began to circle them as he'd demanded, and the weird thing was that once she'd banished her inhibitions, she started to *feel* sexy. She imagined it was Ariston's hands tracing erotic movements over her aroused flesh. She wriggled impatiently and her heavy eyelids fluttered to a close.

'No.' Another soft order rang out in the moonlit bedroom. 'Don't close your eyes. I want you to look at me, Keeley. I want to see your expression when I make you come. And believe me, I am going to make you come, *koukla mou*. Over and over and over again.'

Keeley's eyes widened because his words were so graphic. So *explicit*. She got the distinct impression he was deliberately demonstrating control over her. Was that the way he liked it? To be totally in charge? To tell her what to do and *show her who was boss*? Her heart started to race because he was naked now, his erection so pale and proud amid the dark curls—and even the daunting dimensions of *that* weren't enough to intimidate her. He walked over to where she stood, removing her hands from her breasts and replacing them with his lips, bending his head to kiss each nipple in turn, the tip of his tongue working expertly on the puckered flesh until she let out a small moan of pleasure.

'I like to hear you moan,' he said unsteadily. 'I promise I'm going to make you moan all night.'

'Are you?'

'Neh.' He tangled his fingers in the spill of her hair, anchoring her head so that she couldn't look anywhere except at him. 'Do you know how many times I have

imagined you like this, Keeley? Standing naked in the moonlight like some kind of goddess?'

Goddess? Was he crazy? A shelf-stacker from Super Save who was carrying too much weight? A wave of hysteria bubbled up inside her. She wanted to tell him not to say things like that but the truth was she liked it. She liked the way it made her feel. And why *shouldn't* she feel like a goddess for once when his words were painting pictures in her imagination which were increasing her desire? Because this was probably the way he did it. His method. Sweet-talking her into submission with his practised lines. Telling her the things she longed to hear, even if they weren't true. Presumably this was what men and women did all the time and it didn't mean a thing. Sex didn't mean a thing. That had been one thing her mother *had* taught her.

'Ariston,' she managed, through bone-dry lips.

'Have you dreamed about me too?' he murmured.

She supposed it would destroy the mood if she admitted that all the dreams she'd had about him were deeply unsettling. But why destroy the mood with an admission which no longer seemed relevant?

'Maybe,' she admitted.

He let out a low laugh of pleasure as he skimmed his hand over her tiny thong. 'I love that you blow so hot and cold,' he said. 'Did you learn long ago how to keep a man guessing?

Keeley bit her lip. His impression of her was a million miles away from the reality, but why puncture the bubble now? He obviously thought she was some kind of man-magnet and surely it would be a waste of time to try to convince him otherwise. Because she wasn't expecting any future in this. She knew that only a fool would expect a relationship with a man like Ariston, but her heart still clenched as she acknowledged just how fleeting it was going to be. And if his fantasies about her were turning him on, why not play the game? Why not scrabble up what little knowledge she had and work with it?

'Do you always waste so much time talking?' she purred.

Her softly spoken tease made the atmosphere change. She could sense a new tension in him as he picked her up and carried her over to the bed, not bothering to pull back the bedsheet as he laid her on it. His eyes were unfathomable as he stared down at her.

'Forgive me for not recognising your...' he slid his hand between her legs, pushing aside the panel of her panties with a murmur of acknowledgment as he flicked his finger over her slick, wet heat '...impatience.'

Keeley swallowed because now his finger was working with a purpose and she could feel the heat inside her building. She wanted him to kiss her again but the only area he seemed interested in kissing was her torso and then her belly and then...then... She sucked in a shocked breath as he pulled down her panties and moved his head between her legs so that she could feel the tickle of his thick hair brushing against her thighs. Her body was tensed for what was going to happen next but nothing on earth could have prepared her for that first sweet lick. She jerked on the bed and tried to wriggle away from the almost unendurable pleasure which was spiralling up inside her, but he was holding her hips so she couldn't move. And so she lay there help- lessly—a willing prisoner of the Greek tycoon as layer upon layer of pleasure built to such a level of intensity that when it broke it felt like a swollen river bursting its banks and she screamed out his name.

As the spasms slowly ebbed away she felt a delicious warmth seeping through her body and opened her eyes to find him leaning over her, a trace of amusement curv- ing the edges of his lips.

'Mmm…' he said softly. 'For a woman who blows so hot and cold, I didn't expect you to be quite so vocal. Are you always so sweetly *enthusiastic* when you come, Keeley—or are you trying to massage my ego by acting like that was the first orgasm you've ever had?'

Keeley wasn't sure how to answer. She wondered if it would be shameful to admit she'd never experienced pleasure like that before and wondered how he would react if he realised just how sketchy her sexual experi- ence was. She licked her lips. Don't frighten him away, she told herself. Why shatter this deliciously dreamy mood with reality? Tell him what he expects to hear. Be the woman you've never dared be before.

'You shouldn't be so good,' she said lazily. 'And then I wouldn't be quite so…*vocal.*'

'Good? Are you kidding? I haven't even started yet,' he murmured.

She swallowed, and suddenly she felt out of her depth. 'I'm not…'

His gaze lasered into her. 'Not what, Keeley?'

She licked her lips again. 'I'm not on the pill or anything.'

'Even if you were, I always like to be doubly sure,' he said, his voice hardening as he groped around in the pocket of his trousers until he'd found what he was looking for.

Keeley watched as he slid the condom on and thought how *anatomical* this all seemed—as if emotion played no part in what was about to happen. She swallowed. Had she really thought it might be otherwise— that Ariston Kavakos might show her tenderness or affection?

'Kiss me,' she said suddenly. 'Please. Just kiss me.'

Ariston frowned as she made her breathless appeal and as he gave himself up to the kiss she'd demanded, his heart clenched. *Hell...* She was so...*surprising.* One minute the cool seductress and the next—why, she was almost *shy.* After making him wait longer than he'd ever had to wait for anyone, she was so sweet in her response. Had she learned at the knee of her mother how best to captivate a man? Had she discovered that keeping them guessing was the ultimate turn-on for men who'd seen everything, done everything and sometimes been bored along the way?

He felt as if he wanted to explode as he stroked her and kissed her and his heart was pounding as he moved over her, sucking in a deep breath of anticipation as, slowly, he entered her. And wasn't the most insane thing that he was almost *disappointed* at the ease with which he thrust into her slick, wet heat? Hadn't he been fantasising about her for so long that he'd allowed himself the ultimate illusion—and hadn't her wild reaction to her orgasm only reinforced that crazy notion? That maybe she was a virgin and maybe he was the first...

But his insanity lasted no longer than a second before he began to relax and to feast himself on all the soft and curvy flesh which was just there for the taking. She was so hot. So tight. He caught his hands under her thighs and hooked her legs around his back, enjoying her little squeals of pleasure as he increased his penetration. He drove into her hard and harder still, deliberately holding back until she could bear it no longer and called out his name again. And then she just went under, her body arching into a tight bow until she let it go with one long and shuddering cry. And wasn't *this* his fantasy? Not some woman she could never be, but Keeley Turner underneath him while he rode her, with those soft thighs tensing as she came all over again. He waited until her soft moans had died away and only then did he allow himself his own release, his heart clenching as the seed pumped hotly from his body and he reminded himself that *this* was what it was all about. The ultimate conquest of a woman who had been haunting him for years. A farewell to something which should have been finished eight years ago.

He fell asleep afterwards and when he awoke it was to find his lips touching one pouting breast. Barely any movement was needed to take the puckered nipple deep into his mouth and to graze it with his teeth and lick it, until she was squirming beneath him and before he knew what was happening he was inside her again. This time it was longer. Slower. As if it were all happening in some kind of dream. But his orgasm just went on and on and on. Afterwards he rolled onto his back, careful to allow her head to rest on his shoulder because women were very susceptible to rejection at times like this—and although he planned to wave her goodbye in the very near future, it certainly wouldn't be tonight. But he needed to think about what happened next because this was a situation which would need unusual levels of diplomacy. His fingertip skated a light survey over her belly and he felt her shiver in response.

'Well,' he whispered. 'I can't think of a more satisfactory end to the evening.'

Keeley nodded, trying not to show her disappointment. Of all the things he *could* have said and he came out with something like that. Why, he made her feel like an after-dinner brandy he'd consumed! She licked her swollen lips. But what did she expect? Words of admiration and affection? Ariston telling her she was the only woman for him and that he wanted a relationship with her? Of course not. It was what it was, she told herself fiercely. A one-night stand which wasn't supposed to mean anything. So she rolled away from him, shaking her tangled hair free as she attempted to find the level of sophistication which this kind of situation no doubt called for.

'Indeed it was,' she agreed coolly.

There was a short silence for a moment, during which he seemed to be mulling over his words.

'I'm surprised Santino didn't try to follow you down here to get to you before I did,' he said eventually.

It was such a random remark that Keeley frowned

as she turned her head to look at him, pushing back a handful of untidy hair. 'Why on earth would he have done that?'

He shrugged. 'I noticed how much attention he was paying you throughout dinner.'

'Did you?' she said, without missing a beat.

'I certainly did. And after you'd gone Santino and Rachel left pretty abruptly too. We could hear them arguing all the way back to their room.'

'And you thought...what?' she questioned softly as some inner warning system began to sound inside her head. 'Did you think it was about me?'

'I suspect it was. Your name was mentioned more than once.'

'And...what?' she demanded. 'Did you think I was hungry for a man, Ariston? Any man? That if Santino *had* arrived before you that I would be in bed with him?'

'I don't know.' There was a heartbeat of a pause as he lifted his eyes to hers. 'Would you?'

Keeley froze just before instinct kicked in and she longed to flex her fingernails over his skin and tear at his silken flesh. To inflict some kind of hurt on him—something which might mimic the searing pain which was clamping around her heart. She expelled the breath she'd been holding, bitterly aware of how little he thought of her. But she'd known that from the start, hadn't she? And had thought, what? That the growing sexual attraction between them would somehow cancel out his obvious lack of respect? That admitting him to her bed so quickly might make him admire her? What a stupid little fool she'd been.

'Get out,' she said, in a low voice.

'Oh, Keeley,' he said softly. 'There's no need to over-react. You asked me a question and I answered it truth-fully. Would you rather I told you a lie?'

'I mean it!' she snapped. He made to pull her back into his arms but she jumped out of bed before he could touch her. 'Get out of here,' she repeated.

He shrugged as he swung his legs over the bed and reached for his trousers. 'I wasn't intending to insult you.'

'Really? In that case, I think you ought to take a good, long look at the things you just said. You think I'm sexually indiscriminate, do you, Ariston? That one attractive man is pretty much the same as any other?'

'How should I know? You are your mother's daugh-ter, after all. And I've had enough experience of women to know what they are capable of,' he said rawly. 'I know just how unscrupulous they can be.'

Keeley reached for the cotton dressing gown which was hanging on a hook on the door and pulled it on, not daring to speak until she had tied the belt around her waist and her naked body was hidden from his gaze.

'Why *did* you seduce me, Ariston?' she questioned in a low voice. 'When you obviously think so little of me?'

He paused in the act of sliding on his shirt, the move-ment making his powerful muscles ripple beneath the silk fabric. 'Because I find you intensely attractive. Be-cause you lit a longing in me all those years ago which never really went away. Maybe now it will.'

'And that's all?'

His eyes narrowed. 'Isn't that enough?'

But instinct told her there was something more. Something he was holding back. And suddenly she needed to know, even though she suspected it was going to shatter her. 'Tell me the truth like you did before,' she said. 'Just…tell me.'

His eyes gleamed like silver in the moonlight, before he shrugged. 'It started out with wanting to have you for myself, for all the reasons I've just stated,' he said in a low voice. 'But also because…'

'Because what, Ariston? Please don't stop now. Not when this is just getting fascinating.'

He zipped up his trousers before looking up. 'Because I knew that my brother wouldn't be tempted by you, if he knew I'd had sex with you first.'

'Which naturally you would have made sure he knew?'

He shrugged. 'If I'd needed to, then yes. Yes, I would.'

There was a disbelieving silence before she could bring herself to respond. 'So it was…it was some kind of territorial thing? The ultimate deterrent to ensure that your brother wasn't tempted, even though there is no spark between me and Pavlos and there never has been?'

He met her gaze unflinchingly. 'I guess so.'

Keeley felt faint. It was even worse than she'd thought. Briefly, she closed her eyes before going into damage-limitation mode and that was something which came as naturally to her as breathing. The thing she was best at. She sucked in an unsteady breath. 'You do realise I'm going to have to leave the island? That I can't work for you any more. Not after this.'

He shook his head. 'You don't have to do that.'

'Really?' She gave a bitter laugh. 'Then how do you see this playing out? Me carrying on with my domestic work while you occasionally sneak down here to have sex with me? Or am I now supposed to abandon my uniform as if this was some bizarre kind of promotion and join you and your guests for dinner every night?'

'There's no need to overreact, Keeley,' he gritted. 'We can work something out.'

'That's where you're wrong, Ariston. We can't. There's no working out something like this. I won't be treated in this way and I won't spend any more time in the company of a man who is capable of such treatment. Tonight was a mistake—but we can't do anything about it now. But I'm not staying here a second longer than I have to. I want to leave tomorrow, first thing. Before anyone is awake.'

He'd finished buttoning up his shirt and the expression on his rugged face was hidden by a series of shifting shadows. 'You're aware that you need my co-operation to do that? That I own the airstrip as well as the planes—and no other aircraft is allowed to land or take off from here without my permission. I might not be willing to let you go so easily, Keeley—have you thought about that?'

'I don't care what *you* want, you'd just better let me go,' she said, her voice shaking now. 'Because I'm a strong swimmer—and if I have to make my own way to the nearest island, then believe me I will. Or I'll contact one of the international newspapers and tell them I'm being kept prisoner on the Greek tycoon's island—I imagine the press could have a lot of fun with that. Unless you're planning to confiscate my computer while you're at it—which, I have to inform you, is a criminal offence. No? So get out of here, Ariston—and prepare one of your planes to take me back to England. Do you understand?'

CHAPTER SIX

ARISTON STARED OUT of the vast windows, but for once the travel-brochure views of his island home failed to impress him. He might as well have been in a darkened cave for all the notice he took of the sapphire sea and silver sand, or the neglected cup of coffee which had been cooling on his desk for the last half-hour. All he could see was a pair of bright green eyes and a pair of soft, rosy lips—and pale hair which had trickled through his fingers like moonlight.

What was his problem? he wondered impatiently as he stood up with a sudden jerking movement which made the cup rattle. Why did he persist in feeling so *unsettled* when all should have been well in his world? Weeks had passed since Keeley Turner had fallen eagerly into his arms during a sexual encounter which had blown his mind but ended badly. She had flown back to London the next morning, refusing to meet his eye and saying nothing other than a tight-lipped good-bye before turning her back on him. But she had taken the money he'd given her, hadn't she? Had shown no qualms about accepting the additional sum he had included. He'd thought he might receive an angry email telling him what he could do with his money—wasn't that what he'd *hoped* might happen?—along with some furious tirade suggesting he might be offering payment *for services rendered*. But no. She was a woman, wasn't she—and what woman would ever turn down the offer of easy money?

And that had been that. He hadn't heard from her since. He told himself that was a good thing—that he had achieved what he had set out to achieve and bedded a woman whose memory had been haunting him for years. But infuriatingly, little had changed. In fact, it seemed a whole lot worse. Surely by now he shouldn't still be thinking about her, or the way it had felt to press his lips to her pulsating heat as she had orgasmed right into his mouth. Was it because he wasn't used to a woman walking away from him, or because he couldn't help admiring the tempestuous show of spirit she had displayed when she had stormed away? Or just because she'd been the hottest lover he'd ever had?

But after yet another disturbed night he found himself wondering where was the closure he'd been chasing and why he hadn't tried a little harder to keep her here a bit longer, so he could have got her out of his system. Should he have softened his answers to her questions with a little diplomacy and told her what she wanted to hear, instead of giving it to her straight? His mouth hardened. It didn't matter. He didn't like lies and it was too late to go back over that now. What was done was done.

At least Pavlos had announced his engagement to

the beautiful Marina, with a wedding planned for early next year. His brother was happy—he'd called him just last night from Melbourne and told him so, and Ariston felt as if his work was done. That all was well within the Kavakos dynasty—its future now ensured…if only this damned disquiet would leave him.

But it didn't leave him, despite a schedule spent travelling across much of Southeast Asia—and although he threw himself into his work even more single-mindedly than usual, he remained as unsettled as ever. Which was why he found himself making an unplanned trip to England on his private jet, telling himself it was always useful to pay an unexpected visit to his London office because it kept his staff on their toes. And besides, he liked London. He kept a fully staffed apartment there which he used at different times during the year—often when the summer heat of Lasia was at its most intense. But even in London he found himself struggling to concentrate on his latest shipbuilding project or enjoy the fact that the company had been featured in the prestigious *Forbes* magazine in a flattering article praising his business acumen.

He told himself it was curiosity—or maybe courtesy—which made him decide to call on Keeley, to see how she was doing. Maybe she'd calmed down enough to be civil to him. He felt the beat of anticipation. Maybe even more.

He had his car drop him down the road from her bedsit and when he knocked on the door, the long silence which followed made him think nobody was home. A ragged sigh escaped from his lungs. So that was that.

He could leave a note, which he suspected would find its way straight into the bin. He could try calling but something told him that if she saw his name on the screen, she wouldn't pick up. And that had never happened to him before either.

But then the door opened a little and there was Keeley's face peering out at him through the narrow crack—her expression telling him he was the last person she had expected to see. Or wanted to see. His eyes narrowed because she looked terrible. Her blonde hair hung in limp strands as if it hadn't been washed in days, her face was waxy white and she had deep shadows beneath her eyes. He'd never seen a woman who had paid such scant attention to her appearance—but then he'd never made an impromptu call like this before. 'Hello, Keeley,' he said quietly.

Keeley stiffened, her knuckles tightening over the doorknob as she stared into Ariston's searing blue eyes and a wave of horror washed over her. What in heavens name was he doing here—and how was she going to deal with it? Her instinct was to slam the door in his face but she'd tried that once before without success and, besides, she couldn't do that, could she? Not in the circumstances. She might despise him but she needed to talk to him and it just so happened that fate had scheduled that unwanted prospect without her having to arrange it herself. She found herself wishing she'd had time to brush her hair or put on clothes she hadn't fallen asleep in, but maybe it was better this way. At least she wouldn't have to worry about him making a pass at her when she looked like this. Why, he must be wondering what had possessed him to take someone like her to his bed.

'You'd better come in,' she said.

He looked surprised at the invitation and she understood why. After the way they'd parted he must have thought she'd never want to see him again. But no matter how much she wished that could be true, she couldn't turn him away—just as she couldn't turn the clock back. She had to tell him. It was her duty to tell him.

Before he worked it out for himself.

'So what brings you here today, Ariston?' she said, once they were standing facing each other in the claustrophobically small sitting room. 'Let me guess... Pavlos is back in London and you've decided to check whether or not I've got my greedy hooks in him. Well, as you can see—I'm here on my own.'

He gave a short shake of his head. 'Pavlos is engaged to be married.'

'Wow,' she said, feeling winded though she wasn't sure why. 'Congratulations. So you got what you wanted.'

He shrugged. 'My wish to see my brother happily settled with a suitable partner has been fulfilled, yes.'

'But if Pavlos is safe from my supposed clutches, then what brings you to New Malden?' She frowned. 'An area like this isn't exactly a billionaire's stomping ground, is it? And I don't recall leaving anything behind on your island which might need "returning".'

'I was in London and I thought I'd drop by to see how you are.'

'How very touching. Do you do that with all your ex-lovers?'

His mouth hardened. 'Not really. But then, none of my lovers have ever walked out on me like that.'

'Oh, dear. Is your ego feeling battered?'

'I wouldn't go quite that far,' he said drily.

'So now you've seen how I am.'

'Yes. And I don't like what I see. What's the matter, Keeley?' His frowning blue gaze stayed fixed on her face. 'You look sick.'

Keeley swallowed. So here it was. He'd given her the perfect opportunity to tell him her life-changing news. She was surprised he hadn't worked it out for himself and if he'd bothered to look harder at her baggy shirt, he might have noticed the faint curve of her belly beneath. She opened her mouth to tell him but something made her hesitate. Was it self-preservation? The sense that once she told him nothing was ever going to be the same?

'I have been sick,' she admitted, before the words came out in a bald rush. 'Actually, I'm pregnant.'

He didn't catch on, not straight away—or if he did, he didn't show it.

'Congratulations,' he said evenly. 'Who's the father?'

It was a reaction she should have anticipated but stupidly she hadn't and Keeley felt hurt. She wanted to tell him that only one man could possibly be the father but he probably wouldn't believe her and why should he? She hadn't exactly acted with any restraint where he was concerned, had she? She'd fallen into his arms—not once, but twice and made it clear she'd wanted sex with him. Why wouldn't a chauvinist like Ariston Kavakos imagine she behaved like that all the time? She licked her lips.

'You are,' she said baldly. 'You're the father.'

His face showed no reaction other than a sudden coldness which turned his eyes into sapphire ice. 'Excuse me?'

Was he expecting his cool question to prompt her into admitting that she'd made a mistake, and he wasn't going to be a daddy after all? That she was trying it on because he was so wealthy? The temptation to do just that and make him go away was powerful, but her conscience was more powerful still. Because he *was* the father—there was no getting away from that and the important thing was how she dealt with it. Suddenly, Keeley knew that, despite her morning sickness and ever-present sensation of feeling like a cloth which had been wrung out to dry, she now needed to be strong. Because Ariston was strong. And he was a dominant male who would ride roughshod over her to get what it was he wanted, if she let him.

'You heard me,' she said quietly. 'You're the father.'

His face darkened as he studied her and suddenly she got an idea of just how formidable an opponent he might be in the boardroom.

'How do you know it's mine?'

She flinched. 'Because you're the only one it could be.'

'I only have your word for that, Keeley. You were no virgin.'

'Neither were you.'

He gave a cruel smile. 'Like I told you—it's different for men.'

'You think I would lie about something like this?'

'I don't know—that's the thing. I know very little about you. But I'm a wealthy man. There are undoubted benefits to getting pregnant by someone like me. So was it an accident, or did you plan it?'

'*Plan* it? You think I deliberately got myself pregnant, just to get my hands on your money?'

'Don't look so outraged, Keeley. You wouldn't believe the things people would do for money,' he said, his gaze flicking over her coldly. 'Or maybe you would.'

'You seem to be very good at dishing out blame, but I'm not going to carry the entire burden.' She sucked in a deep breath as she walked over to the window sill. 'I always thought contraception was the joint responsibility of both parties.'

Ariston met her shadowed eyes and was surprised by a sudden wave of compassion—and guilt. How many times had he made love to her that night? His brow furrowed. Just twice, before she'd kicked him out of her bed and announced that she was leaving the island. Had he been careful that second time, or had he...? His heart missed a beat. No. He hadn't. He'd been so aroused that in his sleepy and already sated state he had slipped inside her without bothering to put on a condom. How the hell had that happened, when he was traditionally always the most exacting of men?

And hadn't it felt beyond blissful to feel her bare skin against his? Her slick wet heat against his hardness. Had some protective instinct made his mind shut down so that only just now was he remembering it?

His heart was thundering as he watched her, noting the way she had slumped against the window sill. When she leaned back like that he could see the curve of her belly and for the first time noticed that her already generous breasts were even bigger than usual. She was undeniably pregnant—so should he simply take her word that he was the father?

But memories of his mother—and many of the women in between—made him wary. He knew all about lies and subterfuge because they'd been woven into the fabric of his life. He knew what people would do for money. He had learnt caution at an early age because he'd needed to. It had protected him from some of the darker things which life had thrown at him and Pavlos, so why shouldn't he seek its protection now?

'You're right, of course. Contraception is the responsibility of the man and the woman,' he said. 'But that still doesn't answer my question with any degree of satisfaction. How do I know—or *you* know—that I'm the father of your baby?'

'Because...'

He saw her bite her lip as if she was trying to hold the words back but then they came tumbling out in a passionate torrent.

'Because I've only ever had sex once before!' she declared. 'One man, one time, years ago—and it was a disaster, okay? Does that tell you everything you need to know, Ariston?'

He felt a dark and primitive rush of pleasure. It all added up now. Her soft sense of wonder when he'd made love to her. Her disbelieving cries as she had come. These all spoke of a woman achieving satisfaction for the first time, not someone who'd been around the sexual block a few times. But what if she was lying? What if she was simply using the skills of an actress, learnt at the knee of her mother? His mouth hardened. Surely he owed it to himself to demand a DNA test—if not now, then at least when the child was born.

But her waxy complexion and tired eyes were making him stall and he was surprised by another wave of compassion. He forced himself to sift through the available facts and the possible solutions. Despite her lack of qualifications, she wasn't stupid. She must realise that he'd come at her with all guns blazing if he discovered he'd been bamboozled by a false paternity claim.

He glanced around the shabby little room, trying to impose some order on his whirling thoughts. Fatherhood had never been on his agenda. He accepted that he was a difficult man who didn't believe in love, who didn't trust women and who fiercely guarded his personal space—and those factors had ruled out the forced intimacy of marriage. The desire to carry on his own bloodline had always been noticeable by its absence and he'd always supposed that Pavlos would be the one to provide the necessary heirs to take the Kavakos empire forward.

But this disclosure altered everything. In a few short minutes he could feel something changing inside him, because if this was *his* child then he wanted a part of it. A big part of it. His heart clenched. For how could it be any other way? Why would he not want to stake a claim on his own flesh and blood? He looked into Keeley's wary eyes and thought this must be the last thing she wanted—an unplanned baby with a man she loathed. And no money, he reminded himself grimly. Her circumstances were more impecunious than most. So why not offer her the kind of inducement which would suit them both?

'So when were you going to tell me?' he demanded. 'Or weren't you going to bother?'

'Of course I was. I was just…waiting for the right time,' she said, with the voice of someone who had been putting off the inevitable. 'Only it never seemed to come.'

He frowned. 'Why don't you sit down in that chair? You don't look very comfortable standing there and you really should be comfortable, because we need to talk.'

Her chin jutted forward but she didn't defy him, though he noticed that she stared straight ahead as she made her way towards a battered armchair. Yet despite her unwashed hair and sloppy grey sweat-pants, Ariston couldn't help his body from reacting as she walked past him. He could feel the tautness and the tension hardening his muscles and the instinctive tightening low in his abdomen. What was it about her which made him want to impale her whenever she came near?

She sank down onto the chair and lifted up her face to his. 'So talk,' she said.

He nodded, sliding his hands into the pockets of his trousers as he looked at her. 'I don't imagine you wanted to be a mother,' he began.

She shrugged. 'Not yet, no.'

'So how about I free you of that burden?'

She must have misunderstood him because her arms

instantly clamped themselves around her belly as if she was shielding her unborn child and suddenly she was yelling at him. 'If you're suggesting—'

'What I'm *suggesting*,' he interrupted, 'is that I have you moved from this miniature hell-hole into a luxury apartment of your choice. That you are attended by the finest physicians in the land, who will monitor your pregnancy and make sure that you both maintain tip-top health. And after the birth...'

'After the birth...*what*?' she said, her voice dropping to a whisper, as if she'd suddenly got an inkling of what he was about to say.

'You give up your baby.' He gave a cold smile. 'Or rather, you give it to me.'

There was a pause. 'Could you...could you repeat that?' she said faintly. 'Just so I can be sure I haven't misunderstood your meaning.'

'I will raise the child,' he said. 'And you can name your price.'

She didn't speak for a moment and he was taken aback by the naked fury which blazed from her green eyes as she scrambled to her feet. For a minute he thought she was about to hurl herself across the room and attack him and wasn't there a part of him which wanted her to go right ahead? Because a fighting woman was a woman who could be subdued in all kinds of ways and suddenly he found himself wanting to kiss her again. But she didn't. She stood there, her hands on her hips, her breath coming quick and fast.

'You're offering to *buy* my baby?'

'That's a rather melodramatic way of putting it,

Keeley. Think of it as a transaction—the most reasonable course of action in the circumstances.'

'Are you out of your mind?'

'I'm giving you the opportunity to make a fresh start.'

'Without my *baby*?'

'A baby will tie you down. I can give this child everything it needs,' he said, deliberately allowing his gaze to drift around the dingy little room. 'You cannot.'

'Oh, but that's where you're wrong, Ariston,' she said, her hands clenching. 'You might have all the houses and yachts and servants in the world, but you have a great big hole where your heart should be. You're a cold and unfeeling brute who would deny your baby his mother—and therefore you're incapable of giving this child the thing it needs more than anything else!'

'Which is?'

'Love!'

Ariston felt his body stiffen. He loved his brother and once he'd loved his mother, but he was aware of his limitations. No, he didn't do the big showy emotion he suspected she was talking about and why should he, when he knew the brutal heartache it could cause? Yet something told him that trying to defend his own position was pointless. She would fight for this child, he realised. She would fight with all the strength she possessed, and that was going to complicate things. Did she imagine he was going to accept what she'd just told him and play no part in it? Politely dole out payments and have sporadic weekend meetings with his own flesh and blood? Or worse, no meetings at all. He met the green blaze of her eyes.

'So you won't give this baby up and neither will I,' he said softly. 'Which means that the only solution is for me to marry you.'

He saw the shock and horror on her face.

'But I don't want to marry you! It wouldn't work, Ariston—on so many levels. You must realise that. Me, as the wife of an autocratic control freak who doesn't even like me? I don't think so.'

'It wasn't a question,' he said silkily. 'It was a statement. It's not a case of *if* you will marry me, Keeley— just when.'

'You're mad,' she breathed.

He shook his head. 'Just determined to get what is rightfully mine. So why not consider what I've said, and sleep on it and I'll return tomorrow at noon for your answer—when you've calmed down. But I'm warning you now, Keeley—that if you are wilful enough to try to refuse me, or if you make some foolish attempt to run away and escape…' he paused and looked straight into her eyes '…I will find you and drag you through every court in the land to get what is rightfully mine.'

CHAPTER SEVEN

As she prepared for Ariston's visit next morning, Keeley stared at her white-faced reflection in the mirror and gritted her teeth. This time she wouldn't lose her temper. She would be calm and clear and focussed. She would tell him she couldn't possibly marry him but that she was willing to be reasonable.

She washed her hair and put on a loose cotton dress and a sudden desire to impose some order made her give her bedsit an extra-special clean—busying herself with mop and duster. She even went down to the local market and bought a cheap bunch of flowers from the friendly stallholder who implored her to, 'Cheer up, love! It might never happen!'

It already had, she thought gloomily as she crammed the spindly pink tulips into a vase as she waited for the Greek tycoon to arrive.

He was bang on time and she hated her instinctive reaction when she opened the door to see him in an exquisite pale grey suit, which today didn't make him look remotely uncomfortable. In fact, he came over as supremely relaxed as well as looking expensive and hopelessly out of place in her crummy little home. She didn't *want* to shiver with awareness whenever she looked at him, nor remember how it had felt to be naked in his arms, yet the erotic images just kept flooding back. Was she imagining the faint triumph which curved those cruel lips of his—as if he was perfectly aware of the way he made her feel? *He can't make you do anything you don't want him to*, she reminded herself fiercely. You might be carrying his baby but you are still a free agent. This is modern England, not the Middle Ages. He can hardly drag you up the aisle against your will.

'I'm hoping you've had time to come to your senses, Keeley,' he said, without preamble. 'Have you?'

'I've given it a lot of thought, yes—but I'm afraid I haven't changed my mind. I won't marry you, Ariston.'

He said something soft in his native tongue and when he looked at her, he seemed almost regretful as he sighed. 'I was hoping it wouldn't come to this.'

'Come to what?' she questioned in confusion.

'Why didn't you tell me about your mother?'

She felt the blood drain from her face. 'Wh-what about my mother?'

His gaze slid over her. 'That she's living in a care home and has been for the last seven years.'

Keeley's lips folded in on themselves because she was afraid she might cry, until she reminded herself that she couldn't afford the luxury of tears—or to show any kind of vulnerability to a man she suspected would seize on it, as a starving dog might seize on a bone. 'How did you find out?'

He shrugged. 'The gathering of information is simple if you know who to ask.'

'But why? Why would you go to the trouble of having me investigated?'

'Don't be naïve, Keeley. Because you are the mother of my child and you have something I want. And knowledge is power,' he added as his sapphire eyes bored into her. 'So what happened? How come a middle-aged woman has ended up living in an institution where the average age is eighty, unable to recognise her only daughter when she visits?'

Without thinking, Keeley grabbed the arm of the nearest chair before sinking into it before her legs gave way, as they were threatening to. 'Didn't your investigators tell you?' she questioned hoarsely. 'Didn't they gain access to her medical records and tell you everything you needed to know?'

'No—they didn't. I don't think it's morally right to do something like that.'

'How dare you talk to me about *morals*?' she bit back. 'I'm surprised you even know the definition of the word.'

'So what happened, Keeley?' he questioned again, more softly this time.

She wanted to tell him it was none of his business but she suspected that wouldn't deter him. And maybe it *was* his business now, she realised, with a wrench to her heart. Because her mother was the grandmother of *his* child, wasn't she? Even if she would never realise that fact for herself. A sudden wave of sadness engulfed her and she blinked away another hint of tears before he could see them. 'So what do you want to know?' she questioned.

'Everything.'

Everything. That was a tall order. Keeley leant her head back against the chair but it took a couple of moments before she had composed herself enough to speak. 'I'm sure you don't need me to tell you my mother's fleeting fame as an actress was quickly re-placed by the notorious reputation she gained after that…' she stumbled on the words '…that summer at your house.'

His mouth hardened, but he didn't comment. 'Go on.'

'When we arrived back in England she was ap-proached by lots of tabloid newspapers and the tackier end of the magazine market. They wanted her to be a torch-bearer for the older woman who was determined to have a good sex life, but in reality they just wanted a gullible fool who could shift a few extra copies in a dwindling retail market.' She drew in a deep breath. 'She talked at length about her different lovers—most of whom were considerably younger. Well, you already know that. She thought she was striking a blow for women's liberation but, in reality, everyone was laugh-ing at her behind her back. But she didn't notice and she certainly didn't let it deter her. And then her looks began to fade…quite dramatically. Too much wine and sun. One crash diet too many.'

She stopped.

'Don't stop now,' he said.

His voice was almost gentle and Keeley wanted to tell him not to talk that way. She'd misinterpreted his kindness once before and she wasn't going to make the same mistake again. She wanted to tell him that she could deal with him better when he was being harsh and brutal.

She shrugged. 'She started having surgery. A nip here and a tuck there. One minute it was an eyebrow job and the next she was having goodness knows what pumped into her lips. She started to look…' She closed her eyes as she remembered the cruelty of the newspapers which had once courted her mother so assiduously. The snatched photos which had been only marginally less flattering than the awful ones she'd still insisted on posing for, usually dressed in something cringe-makingly unsuitable—like leather hot pants and a see-through blouse. How quickly she had become a national laughing stock—her face resembling a cruel parody of youth.

And how ultimately frustrating that she had been too blind to see what was happening to her.

'She started to look bizarre,' she continued, not wanting to appear disloyal but now the words seemed to be rushing to get out because she'd never talked about it before. She'd kept it buttoned up inside her, as if it was *her* shame and *her* secret. 'She met this surgeon and he offered to give her a complete facelift, only she didn't bother to check out his credentials or to wonder why he was offering her all that work at such an advantageous price. Nobody was quite sure of what happened during the operation—only that my mother was left brain-damaged afterwards. And that she never recognised me—or anyone else again. Her capacity for normal living is "severely compromised" is how they described it.' She swallowed. 'And she's been living in that care home ever since.'

He frowned. 'But you visit her regularly?'

'I do. Every week, come rain or shine.'

'Even though she doesn't recognise you?'

'Of course,' she said quietly. 'She's still my mother.'

Ariston flinched at the quiet sense of dignity and grief underpinning her words. Maybe it was inevitable that they made him think about his own mother, but there was no such softening in *his* heart. Bitterness rose in his throat but he pushed it away as he studied the woman in front of him. She looked very different today, with her newly washed hair shining over her shoulders in a pale fall of waves. The shapeless sweatpants and baggy top were gone and in their place was a loose cotton dress. She looked soft and feminine and strangely vulnerable.

'Why don't you tell me what it is *you* want?' he said suddenly.

She met his gaze warily, as if suspecting him of setting up some kind of trap. 'I want my baby to have the best,' she said cautiously. 'Just like every mother does.'

'And you think that living here...' he looked around, unable to hide the contemptuous twist of his mouth '...can provide that?'

'People have babies in all kinds of environments, Ariston.'

'Not a baby carrying the Kavakos name,' he corrected repressively. 'How are you managing for money? Are you still working?'

She shook her head. 'Not at the moment, no.'

'Oh?' His gaze bored into her.

She shrugged. 'I found another supermarket job when I got back from Lasia and then I started getting sick. I eked out the money you paid me but...'

'Then how the *hell*,' he persisted savagely as her words tailed off, 'do you think you're going to manage?'

Keeley swallowed in a vain attempt to stop her lips from wobbling, before drawing on her residual reserves. She'd overcome stuff before and she could do it again. 'Once the sickness has improved, then I can start working more hours. If I need to I might have to move to a cheaper area somewhere.'

'But that would take you further away from your mother,' he pointed out.

She glared at him for daring to point out the obvious but suddenly she couldn't avoid the enormity of her situation. She hadn't even got a buggy or a crib—and even if she had, there was barely any space to put them. And meanwhile Ariston was offering what most women in her situation would snatch at. He wasn't trying to deny responsibility. On the contrary, he seemed more than willing to embrace it. He was offering to *marry* her, for heaven's sake. Whoever would have thought it?

But yesterday he'd wanted her to give him the baby, she reminded herself. *To take her child away from her.* Because he could. Because he was powerful and rich and she was weak and poor. He'd wanted to remove her from the equation—to treat her like a surrogate— and *that* was a measure of his ruthlessness. At least if she was married to him she would have some legal rights—and wouldn't that be the safest place to start from? Staring into the watchful brilliance of his eyes, she repressed a shiver as she realised what she must do. Because what choice did she have? *She didn't. She didn't have a choice.*

'If I did agree to marry you,' she said slowly, 'then I would want some kind of equality.'

'Equality?' he echoed, as if it was a word he'd never used before.

She nodded. 'That's right. I'm not prepared to do anything until you agree to my terms.'

'And what *terms* might they be, Keeley?'

'I would like some say in where we live—'

'Accommodation is the last thing you need concern yourself with,' he said carelessly. 'Don't forget, I have a whole island at my disposal.'

'No!' Her response came out more vehemently than she'd planned but Keeley knew what she could and couldn't tolerate. And the thought of the isolation of his island home and of being at Ariston's total mercy made her blood run cold. 'Lasia isn't a suitable place to bring up a baby.'

'I grew up there.'

'Exactly.'

There was a flicker of amusement in his brilliantine eyes before it was replaced by the more familiar glint of hardness. 'Let me guess, you have somewhere else in mind—somewhere you've always longed to live? A town house in the centre of Mayfair perhaps, or an apartment overlooking the river? Aren't these the places women dream about if money were no option?'

'I haven't spent my whole life plotting my rise up the property ladder!' she snapped.

'Then you are rare among your sex.' His gaze bored into her. 'Lasia is my home, Keeley.'

'And this is mine.'

'This?'

She heard the condescension in his voice and suddenly she was fighting for her reputation and what she'd made of her life. It wasn't much, but in the circumstances hadn't it been the best she could manage? Hadn't she struggled to get even this far? But what would Ariston Kavakos know of hardship and making do, with his island and his ships and the ability to click his fingers to get whatever he wanted? Even her. 'I want to stay in London,' she said stubbornly. 'My mother is here, as you yourself just pointed out, remember? I can't just up sticks and move away.'

He rubbed his forefinger along the bridge of his nose and Keeley watched as he closed his eyes, the thick lashes feathering blackly against his olive skin. Was he wondering how he was going to tolerate a life saddled with a woman he didn't really want, with a mother whose incapacity had been brought about by her own vanity? Was he now working out how to back-pedal on his hastily offered proposal of marriage?

His eyes flickered open. 'Very well. London it shall be. I have an apartment here,' he said, rising to his feet. 'A penthouse in the City.'

Keeley nodded. Of course he did. He probably had a penthouse in every major city in the world. 'Just out of interest, how long do you think this marriage of ours is going to last?'

'The tone of your voice indicates that you think a long-standing union unlikely?'

'I think the odds are stacked against it,' she said. 'Don't you?'

'Actually, no, I don't. Put it this way,' he added softly. 'I don't intend for my child to be brought up by any other man than me. So if you want to maintain your role as the mother, then we stay married.'

'But—'

'But what, Keeley? What makes you look so horrified? The realisation that I am determined to make this work? Surely that is only a good thing.'

'But how can it work when it isn't going to be a *true* marriage?' she demanded desperately.

'Says who? Perhaps we could learn to get along together. Something which might work if we put our minds to it. I have no illusions about marriage and my expectations are fairly low. But I think we could learn how to be civil to one another, don't you?'

'That isn't what I meant and you know it,' she said, her voice low.

'Are you talking about sex?' A trace of sardonic amusement crept into his tone. 'Ah, yes. I can see from your enchanting little blush that you are. So what's the problem? When two people have a chemistry like ours it seems a pity not to capitalise on it. I find that good sex makes a woman very agreeable. Who knows? It might even bring a smile to your face.'

Keeley felt both faint and excited at the way he was

expressing himself—and didn't she despise herself for feeling that way? 'And if I…refuse?'

'Why would you?' His gaze flicked over her body. 'Why fight it when submission is much more satisfactory? You're thinking about it now, aren't you, Keeley? Remembering how good it felt to have me inside you, kissing you and touching you, until you cried out with pleasure?'

The awful thing was that not only was he speaking the truth—but she *was* reacting to his words and there didn't seem to be a thing she could do about it. It was as if her body were no longer her own—as if he was controlling her reaction with just one sizzling glance. Keeley's nipples were pushing against her cotton dress and she could feel a newfound but instantly familiar tug of desire. She wanted him, yes—but surely it was wrong to want a man who treated her the way Ariston did. He had used her as a sexual object rather than someone he respected and something told her he would continue to do so. And wouldn't that leave her open to emotional wounding? Because something told her Ariston was the kind of man who could hurt. Who could hurt without even trying.

'But what,' she continued determinedly, 'what if I decided I couldn't stomach the idea of cold-blooded sex with a man like you?'

'Sex with me is never cold-blooded, *koukla mou*— we both know that. But if you were to persist in such stubbornness, then I would be forced to find myself a mistress.' His face darkened. 'I believe that's what usually happens in these circumstances.'

'In that parallel universe of yours, you mean?' she spat back.

'It's a universe I was born into,' he snapped back. 'It's what I know. I won't consign myself to a sexless future because you refuse to face up to the fact that we are having difficulty keeping our hands off each other,' he said. 'But I will not insult you, nor feel the need to take another woman to my bed if you behave as a wife should, Keeley. If you give me your body then I will promise you my fidelity.'

And then he smiled, a hard, cold smile which suggested he was almost *enjoying* her resistance. As if he were savouring the moment until he was able to conquer her. Or defeat her.

'It's up to you,' he finished. 'It's your call.'

Keeley's heart pounded. The way he spoke about marriage and sex was so *primitive*. He was autocratic and proud and he stirred her up so she couldn't think straight, but deep down she realised she had no other place to go. She remembered his warning about taking her to court to fight for the baby if she tried to oppose him. Some men might have made such a threat lightly, but she suspected Ariston wasn't one of them. But women had rights too, didn't they? He couldn't force her to remain in a marriage if it wasn't working. And he couldn't demand sex from her because it was his marital right to do so. Surely even he couldn't be *that* primitive.

'Very well, I will marry you. Just so long as you understand I'm only doing it to give my baby security.' She tilted her chin to meet the triumphant fire blazing from his eyes. 'But if you think I'm going to be some kind of sexual pushover just to satisfy your raging libido, then you're mistaken, Ariston.'

'You think so?' The smile which flickered at the edges of his lips was arrogant and certain. 'I am rarely mistaken, *koukla mou*.'

CHAPTER EIGHT

'Wow! I'VE NEVER seen a bride wearing red before!' exclaimed Megan. 'Is this some new kind of fashion?'

But before Keeley had a chance to answer the woman who'd lent her the ill-fated dress on Lasia, her brand-new husband leaned forward and spoke for her.

'It's an ancient Greek custom,' said Ariston smoothly, his words curling over her skin like dark smoke. 'Traditionally, the bride wore a red veil in order to ward off evil spirits. But I suspect Keeley has deliberately adapted the look and given it a modern twist by wearing a crown of scarlet roses to match her dress. Isn't that right, Keeley?'

Resenting his perception even more than the way he'd just butted in, Keeley looked up into the blue blaze of Ariston's eyes, trying not to react as he slipped his arm around her waist and pulled her closer, looking for all the world like a loving and attentive groom. How appearances could deceive, she thought bitterly. Because he was not a loving groom—he was a cold-hearted control freak who was positively *glowing* with satisfaction because an hour earlier he had slipped an embellished golden wedding ring onto her rigid finger. He'd got exactly what he wanted and she was now his wife, stuck in an unwanted marriage he was determined would last.

He dipped his mouth to her ear and she hated the involuntary shiver which trickled down her spine as his breath fanned her skin.

'Clever you for researching Greek customs so thoroughly,' he murmured. 'Am I the evil spirit you're trying to ward off, Keeley?'

'Of course!' she said, curving her mouth into a big smile, because she'd discovered she could do the appearance thing just as well as Ariston. She could play the part of the blushing bride to perfection—all it took was a little practice. And why spoil a day with something as disappointing as the truth? Why not let people believe what they wanted to believe—the fairy-tale version of their story—that the struggling daughter of a notorious actress had bagged one of the world's most eligible men?

In the back of her mind she'd wondered if her past might catch up with her and if Ariston would have second thoughts about marrying a woman with a history like hers. Yet when a newspaper had regurgitated the old story of Keeley's mother cavorting on the back seat of the ministerial limo and asked Ariston whether the tawdry behaviour of his new mother-in-law gave him any cause for concern, he had broken the habit of a lifetime and given them a quote: 'Old news,' he'd commented, in a bored and velvety drawl. 'And old news is so dull, don't you think?'

Which was kind of ironic when Keeley thought about

how much fuss he'd made about what had happened in the past. But she supposed her pregnancy changed everything. It made him overlook her mother's transgressions. It made him act proprietorially towards her, something which he made no attempt to hide. She could feel him stroking his finger across the front of her scarlet dress, lingering lightly over the curve of her belly as if it was his right to do so. And she guessed it was. Because he was pulling the strings now, wasn't he? Certainly the purse strings. He had given her a brand-new credit card and told herself to buy what she liked—to transform herself into the woman who would soon become his wife. 'Because I want you to *look* like my wife from now on.' His eyes had glittered like blue ice as he had spoken. 'Not some little supermarket stacker who just happens to be wearing my ring.'

His remark had riled her and she'd been tempted to wear her oldest clothes all the time and see how he liked *that*. Would such defiance make him eager to be rid of her and thus grant her the freedom she craved? But then she thought about her baby…and the fact that she was soon going to be a mother. Did she really want to be seen pushing her buggy around the fancy places which Ariston frequented, wearing clothes which had come from the thrift shop? Wouldn't that whittle away at her confidence even more?

But the disturbing thing was that once she'd started, she'd found it surprisingly easy to spend her billionaire fiancé's money. Perhaps there was more of her mother in her than she'd thought. Or maybe she'd just forgotten the lure of wealth and how it could make people do unpredictable things. During her childhood when they'd been flush, money had trickled through her mother's fingers like sand and sometimes, if she'd been feeling especially benevolent, she had spent some of it on her only child. But her gifts had always failed spectacularly. Keeley had been given impractical frilly dresses which had made her stand out from the other little girls in their dungarees. There had been those frivolous suede shoes, ruined by their first meeting with a puddle—and ribbons which had made her look like some throwback to an earlier age. No wonder she'd grown up to be such a tomboy.

But she took to her new credit card like a duck to water, shopping for her imminent role as Ariston's wife with enthusiasm and allowing herself to be influenced by the friendly stylist who had been assigned to her by the fancy department store. She bought new clothes chosen specially to accommodate her growing frame, as well as new underwear, shoes and handbags. And didn't she enjoy the feeling of silk and cashmere brushing against her skin instead of the scratchy qualities of the man-made fabrics she'd worn up till then? She told herself she was only doing what she'd been instructed to do, but the speculative rise of Ariston's dark eyebrows when his driver had staggered into the City apartment under the weight of all those shiny shopping bags had left her feeling...uncomfortable. As if she'd just affirmed some of his deeply held prejudices about women.

But money was liberating, she realised. It gave her choices which had previously been lacking in her life and that newfound sense of liberation encouraged her to buy the scarlet silk dress and matching shoes, secretly enjoying the stylist's shocked reaction when she explained it was for her wedding day.

'You're some kind of scarlet woman, are you?' the woman had joked drily.

And now, at the small but glittering reception, Keeley realised that Ariston's hold on her had changed and he was pushing her away by a fraction so his gaze could rake over her, those smouldering blue eyes taking in every centimetre of the scarlet silk which was clinging to her curves.

'Spectacular,' he murmured. 'Quite...spectacular.'

She felt exposed—almost naked—which hadn't been her intention at all. She felt aroused, too—and surely that was even more dangerous. She tilted her chin defiantly, trying to swamp the sudden rush of desire which was making her skin grow heated and her nipples hard. 'So you approve of my wedding dress?'

'How could I not approve? It would have been entirely inappropriate for such an obviously pregnant wife to wear virginal white.' He gave a slow smile. 'Yet despite your unconventional colour choice and what I suspect was your intention to rile me, let me tell you that you really do make a ravishing bride, Keeley. Glowing, young and intensely fecund.'

'I'll... I'll take that as a compliment,' she stumbled, the tone of his voice making her momentarily breathless.

'That's what it was intended to be.' His eyes narrowed. 'So how are you feeling, *wife*?'

Keeley wasn't quite sure how to answer, because

the truth was complex—and strange. For the first time in her life she actually felt *safe*—and cosseted. She realised that Ariston would never let anyone harm her. That he would use his strength to protect her, no matter what. But he wasn't doing it for *her*, she reminded herself. He was doing it because she was carrying the most precious of cargoes, and as custodian of his unborn child she merited his care and attention. *That* was why he was suddenly being so considerate—and if she read anything more into it than that, then she would be embarking down a very perilous road.

'I'm a little tired,' she admitted. 'It's been a long day and I wasn't expecting it to be such…such an occasion.'

He frowned. 'You want to skip the meal and go home?'

'How can I? It wouldn't look very good if the bride didn't turn up for her own wedding breakfast.'

'You think I care?' He reached out to stroke his fingertips beneath her eyes. 'Your welfare supersedes everything.'

'No, honestly. I'm fine.' The touch of his fingers was doing crazy things to her heart and as she noticed Megan hovering close by with a camera phone pointed in their direction, something made her want to maintain the whole myth of this marriage. Was it pride? She forced a smile as the phone flashed. 'Let's join the others,' she said. 'Besides, I'm hungry.'

But Keeley's reluctance to leave the reception wasn't just about hunger. She was dreading returning to Ariston's gleaming apartment as man and wife and not just because she'd found its vast and very masculine interior intimidating. She had been staying at the famous Granchester Hotel while all the necessary pre-wedding paperwork was completed, because Ariston had insisted that they would only share a home as man and wife. Which seemed slightly bizarre since her rapidly increasing girth made a mockery of such old-fashioned sensibilities. But at least it had given her some breathing space and the chance to get used to her new life without Ariston's distracting presence. She knew she couldn't keep putting off living with him but now the moment of reckoning was approaching, she was terrified. Terrified about sharing an apartment with him and unsure how she would cope. At times she felt more like a child than a grown woman who would soon have a child of her own. Was that normal? she wondered.

But she pushed her reservations aside as she sat down to the Greek feast which had been provided by the hotel and it was a relief to be able to eat after what seemed like weeks of sickness. She could feel her strength returning as she worked her way through the delicious salads, though she could manage only half of one of the rich baklava cakes which were produced at the end of the meal. Despite the relatively small guest list, it somehow managed to feel like a real wedding and Ariston had even asked if she wanted her mother there. Keeley had been torn by his unexpected suggestion. She had felt a wave of something symbolic at the thought of her mother witnessing her marriage, until a last-minute chest infection had put paid to the idea. And maybe that was best. Even if she *had* been aware of what was going on around her, what would her mum have cared about seeing her married, when she'd made such a mockery of marriage herself?

Keeley had wondered why Ariston hadn't suggested a short trip to the register office with the minimum fuss and no guests other than a couple of anonymous witnesses gathered from the street. Wouldn't that have been more appropriate in the circumstances? But his reply had been quietly emphatic.

'Maybe I want to make a statement.'

'A statement?'

'That's right. Shout it from the rooftops. What is it they say? Fake it to make it.'

'By putting your stamp on me, you mean?' she questioned acidly. 'Branding me as a Kavakos possession—just like you did the night you had sex with me?'

His eyes had glittered like sunlight on a dark Greek sea. 'Humour me, Keeley, won't you? Just this once.'

And somehow she had done exactly that. She'd even managed to smile when he stood to make a speech, his fleeting reference to shotguns getting an affectionate laugh, especially from his brother.

'It's funny,' Pavlos said afterwards, with a bemused shake of his head. 'Ariston always vowed he would never marry and he said it like he really meant it. I'd never have guessed there was anything going on between you two. Not after that day at the art gallery when you could have cut the atmosphere with a knife.'

And Keeley didn't have the heart to disillusion him. She wondered what he'd say if he realised that Ariston had bedded her simply to ensure that Pavlos would never want her for himself, and that she had been too stupid and weak to resist him. Yet his need to control had backfired on him because he was now saddled to a woman he didn't really want, though he hid it well. As he raised his glass to toast his new bride, Keeley should have resented his ability to put on such a convincing show of unity—but the reality was a stupid, empty ache in her heart as she found herself yearning for something which could never be hers. He looked like a groom and acted like a groom—but the cold glitter in his blue eyes told its own story.

He will never care for you, she told herself. So don't ever forget it.

During the drive to his apartment, she tugged the scarlet flowers from her head and shook little bits of confetti from her blonde hair. But she couldn't shake off her detachment as she and Ariston walked into the impressive foyer of his apartment building, where doormen and porters sprang to instant attention and a few men in suits shot her bemused glances. She hugged her pashmina around her shoulders in a vain attempt to hide as much of the scarlet dress as possible. Why on earth hadn't she changed into something more sensible first?

A private elevator zoomed them up to the penthouse suite, with its impressive views over many of London's iconic buildings and its seemingly endless suites of rooms. There was even a swimming pool and a gym in the basement—and the outside terraces were filled with a jungle of plants which temporarily made you forget that you were in the heart of the city. She had been there only once before—an awkward visit to oversee the installation of her new clothes in a large room which was now called her dressing room and where every item had been hung in neat and colour-coordinated lines by Ariston's housekeeper.

She hugged the pashmina as they stood in a hallway as big as her bedsit, where a marble statue of a man appeared to be glaring at her balefully.

'So now what do we do?' she said bluntly.

'Why don't you go and change out of that dress?' he suggested. 'You've been shivering since we left the reception. Come with me and I'll remind you where our bedroom is.'

Our? She looked up at him. Had he mentioned that to her before, or had she just not been concentrating? Probably not. His housekeeper had been hovering helpfully during her previous visit, so maybe it had only been alluded to. 'You mean we're going to be…sharing?'

'Don't be naïve, Keeley.' He glittered her a smile. 'Of course we are. I want to have sex with you. I thought I'd made that clear. That, surely, is the whole point of being man and wife.'

'But the vows we made weren't real.'

'No? Then we could make them real. Remember what I said about faking it to make it?' He gave an odd kind of laugh. 'And don't widen your eyes at me like that, *koukla mou*. You look like one of those women in an old film who has been tied to the railway line and only just noticed the train approaching. I don't intend behaving like a caveman, if that's what concerns you.'

'But you said—'

'I said I wanted to have sex with you. And I do. But it has to be consensual. You would need to give yourself to me wholeheartedly—and consciously,' he added with a cool smile. 'I'm not talking about one of those middle-of-the-night encounters, where two bodies collide…and before you know it we're having mind-blowing sex without a single word being exchanged.'

'You mean…' the tip of her tongue snaked over her top lip as she followed him along the corridor, to a room which contained a vast bed which reminded her of a sacrificial altar '…like the night our child was conceived?'

He gave a short laugh. 'That's exactly what I mean. But this time I want us both to be fully aware of what's happening.' There was a pause as he turned around to face her. 'Unless silent submission is what secretly turns you on?'

'I already told you—I have practically no experience of sex,' she said, because suddenly it became important that he stopped thinking of her as some kind of stereotype and started treating her like a real person. 'I…' She bit her lip and said it before she had time to think about the consequences. 'I'd never even had an orgasm before I slept with you.'

He looked at her and she could see a glint of something incomprehensible in his narrowed blue eyes.

'Maybe that's the reason why I'm not trying hard to seduce you,' he said unexpectedly. 'Maybe I want you to stop staring at me as if I was the big, bad wolf and to relax a little. Your dressing room is next door—so why don't you get out of your wedding dress and slip into something more comfortable?'

'Like…what?'

'Whatever makes you feel good. But don't worry,'

he said drily. 'I'm sure I'll be able to keep my hands off you, if that's what you want.'

'That's what I want,' she said, seeing his tight smile before he turned away and closed the door behind him. And wasn't human nature a funny thing? She'd been gearing herself up to fight off his advances, but the news that he wasn't actually going to make any left her with a distinct feeling of *disappointment*. She never knew where she stood with him. She felt as if she were walking along an emotional tightrope. Was that intentional—or just the way he always was around women? She undid the side zip of the red wedding dress, trying to get her head around the fact that this vast room with its amazing views over the darkening city was *hers*.

No. Not hers. His. He owned everything. The dress she stood in and the leather shoes she gratefully kicked off.

But not the child in her belly, she reminded herself fiercely as she walked into the gleaming en-suite bathroom. That child was hers, too.

Stripping off and piling her hair on top of her head, she ran a deep bath into which she poured a reckless amount of bath oil, before sinking gratefully into the steamy depths. It was the first time all day that she'd truly relaxed and she lay there for ages, studying the changing shape of her body as the scented water gradually cooled and she was startled by the sound of Ariston's voice from the other side of the bathroom door.

'Keeley?'

Instantly her nipples hardened and she swallowed. 'I'm in the bath.'

'I gathered that.' There was a pause. 'Are you coming out any time soon?'

She pulled out the plug and the water began to drain away. 'Well, I'm not planning on spending the night in here.'

She towelled herself dry and tied her damp hair in a ponytail. Then she pulled on a pair of palest grey sweatpants and a matching cloud-like cashmere sweater and found her way back through the maze of corridors to the sitting room, where the lights on the skyscrapers outside the enormous windows were beginning to twinkle like stars. Ariston had removed his tie and shoes and he lay on the sofa, leafing his way through a stack of closely printed papers. His partially unbuttoned white shirt gave a provocative glimpse of his chest and, with his long legs stretched out in front of him, his powerful body looked relaxed for once. He glanced up as she walked in, the expression on his shuttered face indefinable.

'Better?'

'Much better.'

'Stop hovering by the door like a visitor. This is your home now. Come and sit down. Can I get you anything? Some tea?'

'That would be great.' She thought how *formal* they sounded—like two total strangers who had suddenly found themselves locked up together. But wasn't that exactly what they were? What did she really *know* about Ariston Kavakos other than the superficial? She realised she'd been expecting him to ring a discreet bell and for his housekeeper to come scurrying from some unseen corner to do his bidding, just as she'd done on her previous visit. But to her surprise, he rose to his feet.

'I'll go and make some.'

'You?'

'I'm perfectly capable of boiling a kettle,' he said drily.

'But...isn't your housekeeper here?'

'Not tonight,' he said. 'I thought it might be preferable to spend the first night of our honeymoon alone and without interruption.'

Once he'd gone Keeley sank down on a squashy sofa, feeling relieved. At least she would be able to relax without the silent scrutiny of his domestic staff who might reasonably wonder why one of their number was now installed as their new mistress.

She glanced up as Ariston returned, carrying a tray, with peppermint tea for her and a glass of whisky for himself. He sat down opposite her and as he sipped his whisky she thought about all the contradictory aspects of his character which made him such an enigma. And suddenly she found herself wanting to know more. *Needing* to know more. She suspected that in normal circumstances he would bat off any questions she might have, with the impatience of a man who held no truck with questions. But these weren't normal circumstances and surely it wasn't possible to co-exist with a man she didn't really know? A man whose child she carried in her belly. She'd *humoured him* as he had requested earlier in the day, so wasn't it his turn to do the same for her?

'You remember asking whether I wanted my mother at the wedding?' she said.

His eyes narrowed. 'I do. And you told me she wasn't well enough to attend.'

'No. That's right. She wasn't.' She drew in a deep breath. 'But you didn't even mention your own mother and I suddenly realised I don't know anything about her.'

His fingers tightened around his whisky glass. 'Why should you?' he questioned coolly. 'My mother is dead. That's all you need to know.'

A few months ago, Keeley might have accepted this. She had known her place in society and had seen no reason to step off the humble path which life had led her down. She'd made the best of her circumstances and had attempted to improve them, with varying degrees of success. But things were different now. *She* was different. She carried Ariston's child beneath her heart.

'Forgive me if I find it intolerable to be fobbed off with an answer like that.'

'And forgive me if I tell you it's the only answer you're getting,' he clipped back.

'But we're married. It's funny.' She drew in a deep breath. 'You talk so openly—so unashamedly—about sex yet you shy away from intimacy.'

'Maybe that's because I don't *do* intimacy,' he snapped.

'Well, don't you think you ought to try? We can't keep talking about cups of tea and the weather.'

'Why are you so curious, Keeley? Do you want something to hold over me?' He slammed his whisky glass down on a nearby table so that the amber liquid sloshed around inside the crystal. 'Some juicy segments of information to provide you with a nice little nest egg should ever you wish to go to the papers?'

'You think I'd stoop to something as low as that?'

'You already did when you wanted to leave Lasia, remember? Or are you blaming a suddenly defective memory on your hormones?'

It took a moment or two for Keeley to recall her blustering bravado, spoken when she'd been swamped by humiliation and the realisation that he'd had sex with her for all the wrong reasons. 'That was then when you were intimating that you might not allow me to leave your island,' she retorted. 'This is now...and I'm having your baby.'

'And that changes things?' he demanded.

'Of course it does. It changes *everything*.'

'How?'

She licked her lips, feeling as if she were on trial, wishing her gaze wouldn't keep straying towards his hands and wishing they would touch her. 'What if our little boy...?' She saw his face change suddenly and dramatically. Saw the same look of fierce pride darkening his autocratic features, as it had done when the sonographer had skated a cold paddle over her jelly-covered bump and pointed out the unmistakable outline of their baby son. For a man who claimed not to do emotion it had been a startling about-turn.

'What if our little boy should start asking me questions about his family, as children do?' she continued. 'Isn't it going to be damaging if I can't answer a simple query about his grandma just because his daddy is uptight and doesn't *do* intimacy? Because he insists on keeping himself hidden away and won't even tell his wife?'

'I thought you said our vows weren't real?'

She met his eyes. 'Fake it to make it, remember?'

There was a pause. He picked up his glass and took a long mouthful of whisky before putting it down again. 'What do you want to know?' he growled.

There were a million things she could have asked him. She was curious to know what had made him so arrogant and controlling. Why he possessed a stony quality which made him seem so *distant*. But maybe the question she was about to ask might give her some kind of insight into his character. 'What happened to her, Ariston?' she questioned slowly and watched his face darken. 'What happened to your mother?'

CHAPTER NINE

ARISTON'S HEART PUMPED violently as he looked into the grass-green of Keeley's eyes. And although deep down he knew she had every right to ask about his mother, every instinct he possessed urged him not to tell her. Because if he told her he would reveal his inner self to her, and that was something he liked to keep locked away.

He understood where his aversion to intimacy stemmed from but was content to maintain that state of affairs. He made the rules which governed his life and if other people didn't like them, that was too bad. His demanding lifestyle had suited him perfectly and, although his lovers had accused him of being cold and unfeeling, he'd seen no reason to change. He'd been self-sufficient for so long that it had become a habit.

Not even Pavlos knew about the dark memories which still haunted him when he was least expecting them. Especially not Pavlos—because hadn't protecting his brother been second nature to him and the highest thing on his list of priorities? But here was Keeley, his new and very pregnant wife, her face all bright and curious as she asked her question. And this wasn't some boardroom where he could quash any unwanted topic at a moment's notice, or a lover he could walk away from without a backward glance because she was being too intrusive. This was just him and her—a woman he was now legally tied to—and there was no way he could avoid answering.

He stared at her. 'My mother left us.'

She nodded and he could see the effort it took her to react as if he'd said nothing more controversial than a passing reference to the weather. 'I see. Well, that's... unusual, because usually it's the man who goes, but it's by no means—'

'No.' Impatiently he interrupted her. 'You want the truth, Keeley? The plain, unvarnished truth? Only I warn you, it's shocking.'

'I'm not easily shocked. You forget that my own mother pretty much broke every rule in the book.'

'Not like this.' There was a pause. 'She sold us.'

'She *sold* you?' Keeley's heart began to slam against her ribcage. 'Ariston, how is that even possible?'

'How do you think it's possible? Because my father offered her a big, fat cheque to get out of our lives and stay out, she did exactly that.'

'And she...never came back?'

'No, Keeley. She never came back.'

She blinked at him uncomprehendingly. 'But...*why*?'

Behind the hard set of his lips, Ariston ground his teeth, wishing she would stop now. He didn't want to probe any more because that would start the pain. The bitter, searing pain. Not for him, but for Pavlos—the little baby whose mama didn't want him enough to fight for him. He felt his heart clench as he started to speak and the bitter words just came bubbling out.

'I'm not saying my father was blameless,' he said. 'Far from it. He'd been brought up to believe he was some kind of god—the son of one of the wealthiest ship-owners in the world. He was what is known as a *player*, in every sense of the word. At a time when free love was common currency, there were always women—lots of women. From what I understand my mother decided she couldn't tolerate his infidelities any more and told him she'd had enough.'

'Right,' she said cautiously. 'So if that was the case, then why didn't she just divorce him?'

'Because he came up with something much more at-tractive than a messy divorce. He offered her a king's ransom if she would just walk away and leave us alone. A clean break, he called it. Better for him. Better for her. Better for everyone.' His mouth twisted. 'All she had to do was sign an agreement saying that she would never see her two sons again.'

'And she…signed it?'

'She did,' he affirmed grimly. 'She signed on the dotted line and went to live a new life in America, and that was the last we ever saw of her. Pavlos was…'

There was a pause and when he spoke it was in a voice devoid of all nuance. A voice, thought Keeley, which was enough to break your heart in two.

'Just a baby,' he finished.

'And you?'

'Ten.'

'So what happened? I mean, after she'd gone.'

He stood up, picking up his papers and stacking them on a nearby table, carefully aligning all the corners into a neat pile before answering her question. 'My father was busy celebrating the completion of what to him seemed like the perfect deal—being completely rid of an irritant of an ex-wife. In his absence he employed a series of nannies to look after us, but none of them could take the place of our mother. Even though I was a child I suspected that most of them had been chosen on account of their looks, rather than their ability to look after a confused and frightened little baby.'

He stared into space. 'I was the one who took care of Pavlos, right from the start. He was my responsibility. I wasn't going to risk anyone else getting close to him and leaving him again. So I bathed him and changed his nappies. I taught him how to swim and to fish. I taught him everything I knew—everything that was decent and good—because I wanted him to grow up to be a normal little boy. And when the time was right, I insisted he go to school in Switzerland because I wanted him as far away from my father's debauched lifestyle as possible. That's why I encouraged him to become a mariner afterwards, because when you're away at sea you don't get influenced or seduced by wealth. There's nothing around you but the wind and the ocean and the wildness of nature.'

And suddenly Keeley understood a lot more about Ariston Kavakos. What had seemed like an overprotective attitude towards his younger brother and his need to control now became clear, because as a child he had seen their lives dissolve into total chaos. That explained his reaction when he'd seen her with Pavlos because for him she had been her mother's child, and a harmful influence. He must have seen all his hard work threatened—his determination that Pavlos should have a decent, normal life about to go up in smoke.

And she understood why he had threatened to fight her for their child too, no matter how ruthless that might seem. Because Ariston didn't actually *like* women, and who could blame him? He was under no illusion that women were automatically the *better* parent who deserved to keep the child in the event of any split. He had seen a mockery made of the so-called maternal bond. He'd fought to protect his own flesh and blood in the shape of Pavlos, she realised—and he would do exactly the same for their own son.

Yet could his mother have been all bad? Wasn't he in danger of seeing only one side of the story? 'Maybe she couldn't have withstood your father's power if she'd attempted to fight for custody,' she ventured.

His voice was like stone. 'She could at least have *tried*. Or she could have visited. Wrote a letter. Made a phone call.'

'She wasn't depressed?' she said desperately, casting around for something—anything—to try to understand what could have motivated a woman to leave her baby behind like that. And her ten-year-old son, she reminded herself. Who had grown into the man who stood before her. The powerful man whose heart was made of stone. Had everyone been so busy looking out for the motherless little baby, that they'd forgotten his big brother must also be lost and hurting?

'No, Keeley, she wasn't depressed. Or if she was she hid it well behind her constant round of partying. I wrote to her once,' he said. 'Just before Pavlos's fifth birthday. I even sent a photo of him, playing with a sandcastle we'd built together on Assimenos beach. Maybe I thought that the cute little image might bring her back. Maybe I was still labouring under the illusion that deep down she might have loved him.'

'And?'

'And nothing. The letter was returned to me, un-opened. And a couple of weeks later we found out that she'd taken a bigger dose of heroin than usual.' His voice faltered by a fraction and when he spoke again it was tinged with contempt. 'They found her on the bathroom floor with a syringe in her arm.'

Keeley rubbed her hands together, as if that would remove the sudden chill which had iced over her skin. She wasn't surprised when Ariston suddenly walked over to the window, his powerful body tense and alert, his broad shoulders looking as if he were carrying the weight of the world upon them. She wondered if he was really interested in gazing out at the tall skyscrapers, or whether he just didn't want to expose any more of the pain which had flashed across his shuttered features despite his obvious attempt to keep it at bay.

'Poor woman,' she said quietly.

He turned back to face her; his habitual composure was back and his eyes were as cold as a winter sea.

'You defend her? You defend the indefensible?' he iced out. 'Do you think that everybody has a redeeming feature, Keeley? Or just if it happens to be a member of your own sex?'

'I was just trying to see it from a different perspective, that's all.' She sucked in a deep breath. 'I'm sorry about what happened to you and to Pavlos.'

'Save your words.' He began to walk across the vast sitting room towards her. 'I didn't tell you because I wanted your sympathy.'

'No?' A shiver ran down the length of her spine as he approached. 'Then why *did* you tell me?'

He had reached her now and Keeley's breath caught in her throat because he was close. Close enough to touch—and she wanted him to touch her. So much. He was towering over her and she could detect the anger simmering darkly from his powerful frame.

'So that you recognise what is important to me,' he husked. 'And understand why I will never let my child go.'

She looked up at him, her heart beginning to pound. Yes, she could understand that perfectly, but where did that leave her? Old sins cast long shadows—was she to be punished for the sins of his mother? Would she be simply another woman for him to despise and mistrust—another woman to regard with suspicion? He'd told her unequivocally he wouldn't tolerate a sexless marriage and would take a mistress if he was forced to do so. But he had also promised her his fidelity if she took him as her lover, and she believed him. Why was that? Because she wanted to believe the best in people, or because she was empty and aching and wanted to reach out to him in the only way she suspected he would let her?

She shifted her gaze from the distraction of his handsome face to the hands which were clasped tightly in her lap. She studied the shiny golden ring which sat beneath the gleaming diamonds of her hastily bought engagement ring and thought about what those bands signified. Possession, mainly—but so far there had been no physical possession. He'd put his arm around her after the ceremony but that had been done purely for show. Yet despite everything she wanted him. Maybe even more than ever before—because didn't the things he'd told her just now make him seem more *human*? He'd revealed the darkness in his soul and she'd come to understand him a little better. Couldn't they draw closer to one another as a result? Couldn't they at least *try*?

She wanted to taste the subtle salt of his skin and to breathe in all his masculine virility. She wanted to feel him inside her again. And it was her call—he'd already told her that. She ran her fingertip over the cold diamonds. She could act all proud and distant and drive him into the arms of another woman if that was what she wanted, but something was making that idea seem repellent.

She snaked her tongue over bone-dry lips, because the alternative was not without its own pitfalls. Was he aware that she was crippled with shyness at the thought of trying to seduce a man as experienced as him? All they'd shared so far had been a mindless night of passion with the sound of the sea muffling their cries. It had happened so spontaneously that she hadn't had to think about it—while the thought of having sex now seemed so *calculated*. Was she expected to stand up and loop her arms around his neck—maybe shimmy her body against his, the way she'd seen people do in films? But if she tried to pretend to be something she wasn't—wouldn't he see right through that?

'Ariston?' she said, lifting her gaze to his at last in silent appeal.

Ariston read consent in the darkened pools of her green eyes and a powerful surge of desire shafted through him. He had revealed more to her than to another living soul and instinct told him it would be better to wait until he had fully composed himself before he touched her. Until the dark and bitter memories had faded. But his need was so strong that the thought of waiting was intolerable. How ironic that this woman carried his child and yet he scarcely knew her body! He'd barely explored the lushness of her breasts or stroked the bush of blonde hair which guarded her most precious of treasures. His heart was hammering as he pulled her to her feet and all he could feel was her soft flesh as she melted against him.

'A real marriage?' he demanded, tilting her chin with his fingers so that she could look nowhere but at him. 'Is that what you want, Keeley?'

'Yes,' she said simply. 'Or as real as we can make it.'

But as he pulled the ribbon from her ponytail, so that her hair fell in a pale waterfall of waves, Ariston knew he must be honest with her. She needed to realise that the confidences he'd shared today were not going to become a regular occurrence. He'd told her what she needed to know so she could understand where he was coming from. But she needed to accept his limitations, and one in particular.

'Don't expect me to be the man of your dreams, Keeley,' he husked. 'I will be the best father and husband that I can and I will drive you wild in bed—that much I promise you, but I can never love you. Do you understand? Because if you can accept that and are prepared to live with it, then we can make this work.'

She nodded, her lips opening as if to speak, but he crushed her words away with his kiss. Because he was done with talking. He wanted this. Now. But not here. He saw her startled look of pleasure as he picked her up and began to carry her towards the bedroom.

'I'm too heavy,' she protested, without much conviction.

'You think so?' He saw her eyes widen as he kicked open the bedroom door and too late he realised this was the kind of thing that women built their fantasies around. Well, that was too bad. He could only be the man he really was. Hadn't he warned her what he was and wasn't capable of? He laid her down fully clothed on the bed, but when her fingernails began to claw at his shoulders he gently removed them. 'Let me undress first,' he said unevenly.

His fingers were trembling like a drunk's as he unbuttoned his shirt and he noted that aberration with something like bemusement. What power did she have over him, this tiny blonde with her moon-pale hair and those green eyes which were forest-dark with desire? Was it because beneath that ridiculous fluffy sweater she carried their child—was it that which made him feel powerful and weak all at the same time?

He saw her eyes dilate as he dropped the shirt to the floor and stepped out of his trousers, yet the kind of flippant question he might *usually* have asked about whether she was enjoying the floorshow didn't seem appropriate. Because this felt...different. He felt the hard beat of rebellion. Surely those meaningless vows he'd made earlier hadn't got underneath his skin?

'Ariston,' Keeley whispered and suddenly she was feeling confused—wondering what had caused his face to darken like that. Was he having second thoughts? No. She swallowed. She could see for herself that was definitely not the case, and though she should have been daunted by all that hard, sexual hunger—the truth was that she was shivering with anticipation.

She raised her lips but his kiss was nothing but a perfunctory graze as he slid off the velour sweat-pants and pulled the voluminous sweater over her head, so she was left in nothing but her underwear. And she was glad she'd allowed the stylist to steer her towards the fancier end of maternity lingerie to buy a matching set of underwear which had cost the earth. The front-clipped lilac silk bra clung to her breasts and the matching bikini briefs made her legs look much longer than usual. As his dark gaze raked over her, the look of appraisal on his face made her feel intoxicatingly *feminine*, despite her shape.

His hand starfished darkly over one breast and as she felt the nipple tighten so presumably did he, because a brief smile curved his lips.

'I want you,' he said unsteadily.

'I want you, too,' she whispered.

He leaned over to skim down her little bikini briefs.
'I've never had sex with a pregnant woman before.'

Lifting her bottom to assist him, Keeley gave him a
reproachful look. 'I should hope not.'

'So this is all very...' he undid the front fastening of
her bra so that her breasts came spilling out and bent his
head to capture one taut tipple between the controlled
graze of his teeth '...new to me,' he rasped.

'New to me, too,' she moaned, her head falling back
against the pillow.

He took his time. More time than she would have
believed possible given his obvious state of arousal.
His body was taut and tense as he stroked his fingertips over her skin—as if he was determined to reacquaint himself with this new, pregnant version of her
body. And, oh, didn't she just love what he was doing
to her? He palmed her breasts and traced tiny circles
over her navel with the tip of his tongue. He tangled his
fingertips in her pubic hair and then stroked her until
she squirmed. Until every nerve ending was so aroused
she didn't think she could bear it any more. Until she
whispered his name on a breathless plea and at last he
entered her. Keeley moaned as he filled her with that
first thrust and he stilled immediately, his eyes shuttered as they searched her face.

'I'm hurting you?'

'No. Not at all. You're...' Some instinct made her
thrust her hips forward so that he went deeper still—
because surely that was safer than telling him he was

the most gorgeous man she'd ever seen and she couldn't quite believe he was her husband. 'Oh, Ariston,' she gasped as he began to move inside her.

And Ariston smiled because this was a sound with which he was familiar. The sound of a woman gasping out his name like that. He forced himself to concentrate on her pleasure, to make this wedding-night sex something she would never forget. Because a satisfied woman was a compliant woman and that was what suited him best. His self-control was almost at breaking point by the time she shattered around him, her fleshy body spasming with release, and it was only then that he allowed himself the luxury of his own orgasm. But he was unprepared for the way it ripped through his body like a raging storm or for the raw, almost savage sound which was torn from his throat as he came.

CHAPTER TEN

A SOFT GLOW crept beneath Keeley's eyelids and in those few blurred seconds between sleeping and waking, she stirred lazily. Replete from pleasures of the night and with the musky scent of sex still lingering in the air, she reached out for Ariston—but the space beside her on the bed was empty, the sheet cold. Blinking, she reached for her wristwatch and glanced across the bedroom. Just after six on a Saturday morning and there, silhouetted by the light flooding in from the corridor, was the powerful figure of her husband, fastening his cufflinks. She levered herself up the bed a little. 'You're not going into work?'

He walked into the bedroom, one of the cufflinks catching the light and glinting gold. 'I have to, I'm afraid.'

'But it's Saturday.'

'And?'

Keeley pushed the duvet away, telling herself not to make waves. Hadn't they just had the most amazing night, with the most amazing sex—and hadn't those hours of darkness felt like perfect bliss? So what if he went to work when most of London was still fast asleep and getting ready for the weekend? She told herself that Ariston's dedication to work was the price you paid for being married to such a wealthy man. But it was hard not to feel disgruntled because it would have been nice to have spent the morning in bed for once. To have done stuff like normal newly-weds—moaning and giggling about crumbs in the bed or debating whose turn it was to make the coffee.

But she wasn't a normal newly-wed, was she? She was the wife of a powerful man who had married her solely for the sake of their baby.

She forced a smile to her lips. 'So what time will you be home?'

Reaching for his jacket, Ariston glanced across to where Keeley lay, looking delectably rumpled and oh-so-accessible. Her heavy breasts were spilling over the top of a silky nightgown, which somehow managed to make her look even more decadent than if she'd been naked. She must have slipped it on again during the night, he thought, swallowing down the sudden dryness which rose to his throat. A night when she had been even more sensual than usual, her uninhibited response to his first careless advances leaving him deliciously dazed afterwards.

He'd arrived home with an armful of flowers impulsively purchased from a street seller outside his office, a vibrant bouquet which bore no resemblance to the long-stemmed stately roses usually ordered by one of his secretaries to placate her when he had been held up by a meeting. And Keeley had fallen on them with delight, burying her nose in the colourful blooms and going to the kitchen to put them in water before his housekeeper had shooed her away and taken over the task.

His heart clenched as he remembered the soft flush of colour to her cheeks and the bright glitter of her eyes as she'd risen up on tiptoe to kiss him. He had pulled her onto his lap after dinner, playing idly with her hair until she'd turned to him in silent question and he'd carried her off to their bedroom with a primitive growl of possession. Had he once told her that he didn't play the caveman? Because it seemed that he'd been wrong. And he didn't like being wrong.

He watched as she tucked a lock of hair behind her ears, the movement making her breasts strain even more against the shiny satin of her nightgown, and he forced himself to look away. To align the pristine cuffs of his shirt beneath his suit jacket as if that were the single most important task of the day.

Was she aware of her growing power over him? A shimmer of unease iced over his skin. She must be. Even someone as relatively innocent as her couldn't be oblivious to the fact that sometimes he didn't know what day of the week it was when she turned those big green eyes on him. Perhaps she was trying to extend that subtle power. Perhaps *that* was the reason for the sudden look of determination which had crossed over her sleep-soft face.

'Ariston?' she prompted. '*Must* you go?'

'I'm afraid I must. Anatoly Bezrodny is flying over from Moscow on Monday and there are a few things I need to look at before he arrives.'

There was a pause as she snapped on the bedside light and pleated her lips into a pout which was just begging to be kissed. 'You spend more time at the office than you ever do at home.'

'Perhaps you'd like to dictate the terms of my diary for me?' he questioned silkily. 'Speak to my assistant and have her run my appointments past you first?'

'But you're the boss,' she protested, undeterred by his quiet reproof. 'And you don't have to put in those kind of hours. So why do it?'

'It's *because* I'm the boss that I do. I have to set an example, Keeley. That's why you have a beautiful home to live in and lots of pretty things to wear. So stop pouting and give your husband a kiss goodbye.' He walked over to the bed and leaned over her, breathing in the sexy, morning smell of her. 'You haven't forgotten we're having dinner out tonight?'

'Of course I haven't.' She lifted her lips to his. 'I'm looking forward to it.'

But he thought the kiss she gave him seemed dutiful rather than passionate, which naturally challenged him—because nothing other than complete capitulation ever satisfied him. Framing her face with his hands, he deepened the kiss until she began to moan and he was sorely tempted to give her what she wanted, until a swift glance at his watch reminded him that his car would be waiting downstairs.

'Later,' he promised, reluctantly drawing away from her.

After he'd gone, Keeley lay back against the pillows, blinking back the stupid tears which had sprung to her eyes. What *was* her problem—and why was she feeling so dissatisfied of late? It wasn't as if she hadn't known what she'd been getting herself into when she'd married Ariston. She'd known he was a workaholic and he'd never promised her his heart. He'd been honest from the start—some might say brutally so—by telling her he could never love her. And she had accepted that. *He was giving as much of himself as he was capable of giving*—that was what she told herself over and over. She closed her eyes and sighed. It wasn't his fault if her feelings for *him* were changing...if suddenly she found herself wanting more than he was prepared to give. And allowing those feelings to accelerate was fruitless; she told herself that too. She would be setting herself up for disappointment if she kept on yearning for what she could never have, instead of just making the most of what she *did* have.

So she ate the delicious breakfast prepared by Ariston's cook and told his driver that she didn't need him that day. She thought the chauffeur seemed almost *disappointed* to be dismissed and, not for the first time, she wondered if Ariston had asked him to keep an eye on her. No. She picked up her handbag and checked she had her mobile phone. She mustn't start thinking that way. That really *was* being paranoid.

She thought about going to look at the autumn leaves in Hyde Park, but something made her take the train to New Malden instead. Was it nostalgia which made her want to go back to where she used to live? To stare at the world she'd left behind and try to remember the person she had been before Ariston had blazed into her life and changed it beyond recognition? She found herself walking down familiar streets until at last she reached her old bedsit, and as she stood and looked up at the window she wondered if she was imagining the surreptitious glances of the passers-by. Did she look out of place with her quietly expensive clothes and extortionately priced handbag as she chased the ghosts of her past?

She ate lunch in a sandwich bar and spent the afternoon at the hairdresser's before going home to get ready for dinner, but she was unable to shake off her air of heaviness as the housekeeper let her in. She didn't know what she'd expected from marriage to Ariston, but it certainly hadn't been this increasing sense of isolation. She'd known he was tricky and distant and demanding, but she'd…well, she'd *hoped*.

Had she thought that living together and having amazing sex might bring them closer together? That what had started out as a marriage of convenience might become, if not the real thing, then something which bore echoes of it? Of course she had, because that was the way women were programmed to think. They wanted closeness and companionship—especially if they were going to have a baby. She knew she'd broken down some invisible barrier after he'd told her about the heartbreak of his childhood and she'd prayed that might signal a new openness. After the passion of their wedding night, she'd waited for that openness to happen. And then she'd waited some more.

And now?

Careful not to muss her hair, she pulled a silky black evening dress over her head. Now she was being forced to accept the harsh reality of being married to someone who barely seemed to notice her, unless she was naked. A man who left early each morning and returned in time for dinner. Who slotted in time with her as if she was just another appointment in his diary. Yes, he accompanied her to all her doctor's appointments and murmured all the right things when they saw their baby son high-kicking his way across the screen. And very occasionally they drove out to the countryside or watched a film together—small steps which made her hope that non-sexual intimacy might be on the cards. But every time her hopes were dashed as those steel shutters came crashing down and he pushed her away—Mr Enigmatic who was never going to make the mistake of confiding in her again.

Ariston arrived home in a rush and went straight to the shower, emerging from his dressing room looking a vision of alpha virility, in a dark dinner suit which matched the raven thickness of his hair. He walked over to the dressing table where she sat and began to massage her shoulders—bare except for the spaghetti straps of her black dress. Instantly she felt the predictable shimmerings of desire and her nipples hardened.

'Ariston,' she said huskily as his fingers dipped from her shoulder to caress her satin-covered ribcage.

'Ariston, what? I'm only making up for what I didn't have time for this morning. And how can I prevent myself from touching you when you look so damned beautiful?'

She clipped on an opal earring. 'I don't feel particularly beautiful.'

'Well, take it from me, you are. In fact, I'm tempted to carry you over to that bed right now to demonstrate how much you turn me on. Would you like that, Keeley?'

Did the leaves fall from the trees in autumn? Of *course* she would like it. But using sex as their only form of communication was starting to feel dangerous. The contrast between his physical passion and mental distance was disconcerting and...unsettling. Each time he made love to her it felt as if he were chipping away a little piece of her, and wasn't she worried that soon there would be nothing of the real Keeley left? That she would become nothing but an empty shell of a woman? She fixed the second earring in place. 'We don't have time.'

'Then let's make time.'

'No,' she said firmly, rising to her feet in shoes which probably weren't the most sensible choice for a pregnant woman, but this was the first time she'd met Ariston's colleagues and, naturally, she wanted to impress. 'I don't want to arrive with my cheeks all flushed and my hair all mussed, not when I've spent all afternoon at the hairdresser's.'

'Then perhaps you should skip the hairdresser's next time,' he commented drily as he glanced at the elaborate confection of curls piled high on her head. 'If it puts you in such a bad mood.'

It was one of those stupid little rows which spiralled up out of nowhere and Keeley knew she ought to dispel the atmosphere which was still with them when they got into their car. She wasn't going to improve matters by sulking, was she? Laying her carefully manicured hand on his knee, she felt the hard muscle flex beneath her fingers.

'I'm sorry I was grumpy.'

He turned towards her, the passing street lights flickering like gold over his rugged features. 'Don't worry about it,' he said smoothly. 'It's probably just your hormones.'

She wanted to scream that not everything involved her wretched *hormones*—but she was aware that such a reaction would make a mockery of her words. She stared down at her baby bump instead, before lifting her gaze to his. Why not tell him about what else had been bugging her lately—a practical issue they could address and which might improve the quality of their lives? 'Ariston.'

'Keeley?'

She hesitated. 'Do we have to have quite so many staff?'

His eyes narrowed. 'I'm not quite sure what you mean.'

She shrugged a little awkwardly and began to fiddle with her jewelled handbag. 'Well, we have a housekeeper, a cleaner, a cook, a driver and a secretary—as well as that man who comes once a week to water all the plants on the terrace.'

'And? It's a big apartment. They all have their necessary roles in my life.'

She didn't correct him by reminding him that it was her life, too. Choose your battles carefully, she reminded herself. 'I know that. I just thought that maybe I could, you know…help.'

'Help?' He furrowed his brows. 'Doing what?'

'Oh, I don't know. Chores. *Stuff.* Something to make me feel like a real person who's connected with the world, rather than some sort of mindless doll who gets everything done for her. A bit of cleaning, perhaps. Maybe even some cooking.' She bit her lip. 'But when I offered to peel some potatoes for Maria the other day, she acted like I'd threatened to detonate a bomb in the middle of the kitchen.'

He seemed to be picking each word carefully, like someone selecting diamonds from a barrel of stones. 'Probably because she didn't think it was appropriate.'

'And why wouldn't it be?'

'Because…' He sucked in a breath and made no attempt to hide his sudden irritation. 'You are not on my staff, Keeley, not any more. You are now the mistress of my household and I would prefer it if you acted that way.'

She sat up ramrod-straight. 'You sound like you're *ashamed* of me!'

'Don't be absurd,' he clipped out. 'But it isn't possible to flit between the two worlds—you must realise that. You can't be peeling potatoes one minute, and asking someone to serve you tea the next. You need to be clear about your new role and demonstrate it to everyone else, so nobody gets confused. Do you understand?'

She swallowed. 'I think I'm getting the general idea.'

He caught hold of her hand. 'And things will probably settle down once you've had the baby.'

'Yes, probably. At least that's something I *can* do,' she said lightly.

There was a pause as he circled his thumb over her palm. 'Though we will need a nurse, of course,' he added.

At first she thought she must have misheard him. 'I'm sorry?' she said, but her heart had started to race with some dark and nameless fear as she looked into his face.

'A nurse,' he reiterated. 'A nursery nurse, I believe they're called.'

'But…' She could feel tiny little beads of sweat pricking at her forehead. 'I thought since you'd been so hands-on with Pavlos, you wouldn't want us to have any outside help with the baby. Was I wrong about that too, Ariston?'

She saw his face darken. Was he angry at the mention of his brother's name—for her daring to bring up a subject he had very firmly closed on the night of their wedding?

'Obviously, you will do the lion's share but I shall be out at work for most of the day.'

'And?' she questioned in confusion as his voice tailed off.

His eyes briefly caught the gleam of lights as the car slid to a halt outside the restaurant. 'And we will need a nurse who speaks Greek, so that my son will grow up speaking my tongue. For that is vital, given the heritage which will one day be his.'

His words were still reeling around Keeley's head as they entered the upmarket Greek restaurant—one of very few in central London, or so Ariston informed her as they were led towards the best table in the room. But she didn't care about the stunning *trompe l'oeil* walls painted with bright blue skies and soaring marble pillars, which made you feel as if you were standing in the middle of an ancient Greek temple. She was so reeling at this latest bombshell that she could barely take in the names of Ariston's formidable-looking colleagues or their beautiful wives, who, to a woman, were sleek and dark and polished. She recited their names silently in her head, like a child learning tables. Theo and Anna. Nikios and Korinna.

And of course they all kept slipping into Greek from time to time. Why wouldn't they, when it was their first language? Even though they seamlessly switched to English to include her, Keeley still felt like a complete outsider. And this was what it would be like when she had the baby, she realised as she stared down at her glass of melon juice. She would be on the periphery of every conversation and event. The English mother who could not communicate with her half-Greek child. Who remained on the outskirts like some silent ghost. She swallowed. Unless she did something about it. Started being proactive instead of letting everyone else decide her destiny for her. Since when had she started behaving like such a *wuss*? If she didn't like something she ought to change it.

The men were deep in conversation as Keeley looked

across the table at Korinna, who was playing with her dish of apple sorbet instead of eating it.

'I'm thinking about learning Greek,' Keeley said suddenly.

'Good for you.' Korinna smiled before lifting her narrow shoulders in a shrug. 'Though it's not an easy language, of course.'

'No, I realise that,' said Keeley. 'But I'm going to give it my very best shot.'

She was just returning from the washroom when she crossed paths with the young waiter who had been looking after their table all evening, and he moved aside to let her pass.

'You are enjoying your meal, Kyria Kavakos?' he questioned solicitously.

'Oh, yes. It's delicious. My compliments to the chef.'

'You will forgive me for intruding?' he said, in his faultless English. 'But I couldn't help overhearing you saying you wanted to learn Greek.'

'I do. I'm just trying to work out the best way to go about it.'

He smiled. 'If you like, I could help. My sister is a teacher and she's very good. She teaches at the Greek school in Camden but she also gives private lessons and is very keen to expand. Would you like her card?'

Keeley hesitated as he offered her a small cream card. She told herself it would be rude to refuse such a kind offer and that perhaps this was an example of fate stepping in to help her. They said that working one-to-one was the best way to learn a new language and this could be an empowering gesture on her part. Wouldn't

it be a brilliant surprise for Ariston if he realised she
was making an effort to integrate into a culture which
was so important to him?

She would show him what she was capable of, she
thought. And he would be proud of her.

'Thank you,' she said with a smile, taking the card
from the waiter and slipping it into her handbag.

CHAPTER ELEVEN

ARISTON LET HIMSELF quietly into the apartment to hear the unmistakable sounds of someone slowly reciting the Greek alphabet. He stood very still. They were coming from the music room, which was situated at the furthest end of the penthouse, and they were being spoken by a voice he didn't recognise. He frowned as he heard a second voice stumble over the letter *omicron*— traditionally a difficult letter for non-Greek speakers to pronounce—and suddenly realised that it was his wife who was now speaking. He began to walk along the corridor and the sight which greeted him took him completely by surprise. A beautiful young Greek girl wearing a sweater and a very short denim skirt was standing outlined against one of the giant windows and his wife was sitting near the piano, reading aloud from a textbook. They looked up as he walked in and he saw uncertainty cross over Keeley's features as her words died away.

The smile he gave was intended to be pleasant but his words didn't quite match. 'What's going on?' he questioned.

'Ariston! I wasn't expecting you.'

'Apparently not.' He raised his eyebrows. 'And this is?'

'Eva. She's my Greek teacher.'

There was a pause. 'I didn't know you had a Greek teacher.'

'That's because I didn't tell you. It was going to be a surprise.'

'Look, I can see you must be busy.' Eva was looking at each of them in turn and beginning to gather up a stack of papers before thrusting them hastily into a leather briefcase. 'I'd better go.'

'No,' said Keeley quickly. 'You don't have to do that, Eva. There's still half an hour of the lesson left to run.'

'I can always come back,' said Eva in a bright voice which suggested this was never going to be an option.

Ariston waited as Keeley showed the teacher out, listening to the sound of her rapid returning footsteps before she marched into the room and glared at him.

'What was *that* all about?' she demanded.

'I could ask you the same question. Who the hell is *Eva*?'

'I told you. She's my Greek teacher—isn't that obvious?'

'Your Greek teacher,' he repeated slowly. 'And you found her...where?'

She sighed. 'She's the sister of the waiter who served us the night we went to the Kastro restaurant. He overheard me saying to Korinna that I wanted to learn Greek and so he gave me Eva's card on my way back from the washroom.'

'Run that past me again,' he said. 'She's the *sister* of some random waiter you met in a restaurant?'

'What's wrong with that?'

'You're seriously asking a question like that?' he demanded. 'Think about it. You don't even *know* these people!'

'I do now.'

'Keeley,' he exploded. 'Don't you realise the potential consequences of inviting *strangers* into my home?'

'It's my home too,' she said in a shaky voice. 'Or at least, it's supposed to be.'

With an effort he altered the tone of his voice, trying to dampen down the anger which was rising up inside him like a dark tide. 'I'm not trying to be difficult, but my position is not like that of other men. I happen to be extremely wealthy. You know that.'

'Oh, yes—I know it. I'm never likely to forget it, am I?' she retorted hotly. 'What do you want me to do, Ariston—go around checking that Eva hasn't pocketed one of your precious Fabergé eggs?'

'Or maybe,' he continued, as if she hadn't spoken, 'maybe introducing you to the Greek teacher was simply a clever diversion and the pretty-boy waiter has designs on you himself?'

'You think he has designs on me?' She stood up and gave a disbelieving laugh as she angled her palms over the curve of her belly. 'Looking like *this*? How dare you? How *dare* you say such a thing to me?'

Ariston let her words wash over him but instead of being irritated by her defiance, all he could think about was how ravishing she looked in her anger. Her blonde hair was spilling wildly around her face and her green eyes were spitting emerald fire and automatically he reached out to pull her into his arms. That first contact made her pupils dilate and although she had started beating her hands furiously against his chest, she moaned when he started to kiss her and she moaned some more when he palmed her nipple and felt the tip pushing hungrily against his hand. She kissed him back and her kiss was hot and hard and angry, but the beating of her fists became less insistent. He levered her closer, and jutted his hips so that she could feel just how hard he was and she writhed against him in furious frustration.

Slipping his hand underneath her dress, he felt her bare thigh and as he began to stroke his fingers upwards towards her panties his desire went right off the scale. Just like hers. He could hear the unsteady rush of her breath as she scrabbled at his belt, and as she slipped the notch free he felt as if he might explode. He was rock-hard and the unmistakable scent of her arousal was in the air as his slowly moving fingers reached her panties to discover they were damp. So damp. He groaned again, and so did she as he pushed the taut panel aside and slicked his finger over her honeyed flesh, confident that sex would dissolve the tension between them as it always did. Couldn't he show her who was boss and wouldn't her hungry body accept that, the way it always did? Her arms wound themselves around his neck and he was about to pick her up and carry her over to the *chaise-longue* when suddenly he came to his senses.

'No,' he said suddenly, his heart pounding in protest

as he removed her hand from his trousers and pushed her away.

It took several moments before she spoke and when she did she looked at him in confusion. 'No?'

'I don't want you, Keeley. At least, not right now.'

'You don't?' she questioned, before giving a disbelieving laugh. 'Are you quite sure about that? Isn't that the way you like to settle any kind of disputes we have?'

He suppressed a ragged groan before forcing himself to step away from her. 'I'm not making love to you when we're in this kind of mood,' he said, his voice thick. 'I'm angry and so are you, and I fear I might be more...*physical* with you than I should be.'

'And?'

'And that's probably not the best idea given that you're pregnant.'

Keeley stared into his shuttered features as desire drained from her body, like water from the bathtub, and in its place came a horrible sinking realisation. Because no matter what she did or what she said—no matter how hard she tried or how long they stayed married—Ariston would always remain in command. She could learn Greek until the cows came home but it wouldn't make any difference. She could even try to find out more about ship-owning, but she would be wasting her time. Because what she wanted didn't count. It was what *Ariston* wanted which counted and it always would, because he ruled the roost and had been allowed to do so for years.

He liked her to know her place and to run everything past him first. He didn't like strangers in the house and now she knew that, she would be expected to respect his wishes. Her home had become her prison and her husband the rigid jailer. And the reason he didn't want to make love to her right now was nothing to do with his fears about her pregnancy. The expression on his face was as dark as the time he'd told her about his mother and suddenly she understood why. Because he didn't like the way she was making him react, she realised.

He didn't want to lose control or to be seen to lose control.

And she realised something else, too. That if she stayed, she would spend the rest of her life sublimating herself to *his* desires and *his* whims. The one thing she had asked for when she'd agreed to marry him hadn't materialised. They would never be equals—and what kind of an example would that be for her son?

Smoothing her hands over her hot cheeks, she stared at him. 'I'm done with this, Ariston,' she whispered hoarsely.

He narrowed his eyes. 'What are you talking about?'

'You. Me. Us. I'm sorry. I can't do this any more. I can't stay in this…this *mockery* of a marriage.'

His smile was cruel. She hadn't seen him look at her that way in a long time, but now she was reminded of the essential ruthlessness which lay at the very core of him.

'But you don't have any choice, Keeley,' he said silkily. 'You're pregnant with my child and there's no way I'm letting you go.'

She met the quiet fury in his eyes. 'You can't stop me.'

'Oh, I think you'll find I can,' he said. 'I have the

experience as well as the wherewithal. You have nothing while I have everything. I can get the full weight of any international court to rule in my favour in a custody battle—don't ever doubt that—though it's a path I'd rather not take. So don't make me, Keeley. Why don't we just calm down and recalibrate?' He fixed his steely blue gaze on her. 'Perhaps I *was* a little unreasonable—'

'*Perhaps?*' she demanded and she realised something else, too. That people didn't interrupt Ariston. His power had allowed him to build a wall around himself so high that nobody ever dared try. He'd made up all the rules and everyone else was supposed to just fall in and obey them. And everyone always had—until now. She was the only one who had dared to step out of line, but he couldn't wait to make her step right back in it again. 'You don't get it, do you?' she said shakily. 'This isn't a marriage, Ariston. It's a farce and a prison—and I'm not just talking about your lack of trust or the jailer-like behaviour you've demonstrated simply because I had the temerity to invite someone home!'

'Keeley—'

'No! You will hear me out. You will. Do you want to hear the reality of what it's like being married to you? Of how great it really is? You spend long hours in the office—and when you're back, at best you tolerate me. Guaranteed orgasms and the occasional trip to the theatre don't add up to intimacy, but I guess I shouldn't be surprised, because you don't *want* intimacy. You told me that yourself and at the time I thought I could live with it, or maybe even change it—but now I know I can't. Because you don't care about me, Ariston—

all you really care about is your baby. Sometimes you make me feel like a character in a science-fiction film, someone who is growing your child so that you can take him away from me just as soon as he's born! As if I'm nothing but a damned incubator!'

'Keeley—'

'Will you stop trying to interrupt me?' she yelled. 'When I mentioned that we were completely outnumbered by staff and spoke of my desire to help with a little housework, you looked at me as if I was some kind of freak. So what am I supposed to do all day? Haunt the shops like some well-dressed mannequin while I blitz your credit card?'

'Lots of women do.'

'Well, not me. If you must know, it bores the hell out of me. I had a brief love affair with excessive spending before we got married, but I'm over it now. It's an empty, meaningless existence. I'd rather give the money to charity than keep buying more overpriced handbags!'

'Keeley—'

'I haven't finished,' she continued icily. 'You speak Greek and I can't, which means I would always be the outsider—and when I do use my initiative to take lessons, I get accused of having the hots for my teacher's brother!'

'I hear what you're saying,' he said, sucking in an unsteady breath. 'And I realise I overreacted. Of course you must have lessons if you want them, but at least let me choose someone suitable to teach you. You can't just sign up with the sister of someone you've bumped into at a restaurant.'

'Why not?'

'Because they haven't been vetted,' he gritted out.

It was the final straw and it was at that point that Keeley knew there could be no going back. And no going forward either. Her heart was pounding fit to burst but somehow she kept her voice steady. 'So what am I supposed to do—be stuck in here while you vet anyone I might wish to see? Do you want to build barriers around me as high as the ones you've built around yourself?'

'*Now* who's overreacting?' he demanded.

'I'm not.' She shook her head. 'I thought things might change a little once we were married—but instead of the closeness I foolishly hoped might happen, all I get is anger and suspicion! I feel sorry for you, Ariston,' she added quietly. 'To view the world in such a cynical way means you'll never be happy and that will inevitably spill over into all our lives. And I'm not having any child of mine brought up in an atmosphere like that. I don't want our son to grow up knowing only distrust and cynicism—or to wonder why Mummy and Daddy never show each other any real affection. I want him to have a healthy view of the world, and that's why I'm leaving.'

'Just try,' he challenged softly.

She gave a nod of bitter understanding as she met his darkened eyes. 'Is that your way of saying you'll cut off my funds? Are you going to play the financial tyrant in addition to the emotional one? Would you really go that far, Ariston—after everything you've been through yourself? Well, go right ahead—be my guest! But if you do that I'll go straight to a lawyer and get them to slap a maintenance order on you. Or I'll sell *these*.' She pointed a shaking finger at the cold diamonds which flashed on her fingers, and then at the glittery tennis bracelet which was dangling from her wrist. 'Or *this*. Or if need be, I'll go to the papers. Yes. I'd do that, too. I'd sell my story and tell them what it was like being married to the Greek tycoon. I'd do anything to make sure you don't take my baby away, no matter how much you offer me to disappear from your life. Because I would never ever walk away from my baby and no amount of money could induce me to.' She sucked in a deep breath before her next words came out with a quiet intensity.

'I am not your mother, Ariston.'

She saw him flinch as if she'd hit him, but nothing was going to stop her now. 'Now, if you'll excuse me,' she said, her voice trembling, 'I'm going to pack my things and move out. And if you try to stop me, I'll… I'll call the police!'

His expression was unfathomable as their gazes clashed and she knew she'd pushed him as far as she possibly could. All the things she'd said had needed to be said and she'd meant every word of them, but that small glimmer of hope inside her refused to die. Could he read it in her eyes? Could he see the yearning she suspected still lingered there? The hope that maybe this showdown had cleared the air once and for all and he would let her get close enough to be the wife she really wanted to be. To show him all the love which was in her heart and maybe break down some of those formidable barriers he'd erected around his own. She swallowed. He might not ever be able to love her back, but couldn't he relax enough to *like* her and to *trust* her?

But the moment he opened his mouth she knew she had been wishing for the stars.

'I think, given your current state of hysteria, that you might be better to sleep on it. I will give you some space by moving into a hotel tonight—and hopefully, by morning, you might have calmed down a little.' His voice suddenly softened. 'Because getting yourself into this kind of state can't be good for the baby, Keeley.'

It was the final twist of the knife and Keeley wanted to howl with frustration. And sorrow. That too. She was glad he cared for his unborn son, but suddenly she needed him to care for her, too—and he was never going to do that. Quickly, she turned away from him, terrified he would see the heartbreak on her face or witness the tears which had begun to stream from her eyes as she stumbled her way towards the bedroom.

CHAPTER TWELVE

THE OCTOBER SKY was grey and brooding and Ariston was staring into space when the intercom on his desk buzzed and the disembodied voice of Dora, his assistant, spoke.

'I have Sheikh Azraq of Qaiyama on the line for you on one, Ariston.'

Restlessly, Ariston tapped his finger against the surface of the desk. He had been waiting for the call to confirm a deal he'd worked hard for. A deal which had the potential to increase the company's portfolio by many millions of dollars. He was about to accept the call when his mobile phone started ringing and he saw the name which was flashing up on the screen. Keeley. He felt the urgent crash of his heart and the sudden tightening of his throat.

'Tell the Sheikh I'll call him back later, Dora.'

'But, Ariston...'

It was rare for his assistant to even *attempt* to remonstrate with him but Ariston knew the reason for her unusual intervention. Sheikh Azraq Al-Haadi was one of the most powerful leaders of the desert lands and

one who would not take kindly to his refusal to accept
a phone call which had taken many days of planning
to organise. But one thing he knew without a shadow
of a doubt was that talking to Keeley was more important. His tapping ceased and Ariston's hand clenched
into a tight fist as satisfaction hardened his lips into a
smile. Was she regretting her decision to walk out on
him? Finding that life wasn't quite so straightforward
without the protection of her influential husband? Had
she realised that he'd been right all along and that his
concern about her associates had sprung solely from a
need to protect her? He allowed himself a beat of anticipation. He would accept her back, yes, but she must
understand that he would accept no similar tantrums or
hysteria in the future—for all their sakes.

'Please tell the Sheikh I will move heaven and earth
to arrange another call,' he said firmly. 'But for now I
have someone else I need to speak to, so don't disturb
me until I say so, Dora.'

He snatched up the mobile phone and clicked the
connection, but took care to keep his voice bland and
noncommittal. 'Hello?'

There was a breathless kind of pause. 'Ariston,' came
the soft English voice which made his heart stab with a
strange kind of pain. 'You took so long to answer that
I thought you weren't going to pick up.'

Something inside him was urging him to make an
attempt at conciliation but the anger he'd felt when she
had carried through her threat and walked out on him
had not left him.

'Well, I'm here now,' he said coolly. 'What is it you want, Keeley?'

The tone of her voice altered immediately and the stumbled apology he had been expecting was not forthcoming.

'As I'm having private healthcare, my obstetrician has fitted in an extra check-up for me and I'm due for a scan tomorrow,' she said, her voice now as cool as his. 'And I thought you might like to come. I realise it's very short notice and you might not be able to clear your diary in time—'

'Is that why you left it so late to invite me?'

He heard the unmistakable sound of a frustrated sigh. 'No, Ariston. But since you haven't bothered answering any of my emails—'

'You know I don't like communicating by email,' he said moodily.

'Yes, I realise that.' There was a pause. 'I just… I wasn't sure whether or not you'd want to see me. I thought about sending you a photo once I'd had the scan done, then thought that wouldn't be fair and so I—'

'What time,' he interrupted brutally, 'is it happening?'

'Midday. At the Princess Mary hospital. Where we went before—you remember?'

'I'll be there,' he said, before the voice of his conscience forced the next question from his lips. 'How are you?'

'I'm fine. All good.' He could hear her swallowing. 'The midwife is very pleased with my progress and I—'

'I'll see you tomorrow,' he said, and terminated the conversation.

He sat staring into space afterwards, angry with himself for being so short with her, but what the hell did she expect—that he would run around after her like some kind of puppy? He stared at the sky, whose dark clouds had now begun to empty slanting rods of rain onto the surrounding skyscrapers. After their blazing row he'd spent the night in a hotel to give her time to cool off, returning the following morning and expecting her to have changed her mind. In fact, he'd been expecting an apology. His mouth hardened. How wrong he had been. There had been no contrition or attempt to make things better. Her mood had been flat yet purposeful as she had repeated her determination to move out.

He'd tried being reasonable. He had not opposed her wishes, giving her free rein to move into her own place, telling himself that, if he gave her the freedom she thought she wanted and the space she thought she needed, it would bring her running right back. But it hadn't. On the contrary, she had made a cosy little nest out of her rented cottage on Wimbledon Common, as if she was planning to stay there for ever. During his one brief visit, he had stared in disbelief at the sunny yellow room, which she had made into a perfect nursery by adorning the walls with pictures of rabbits and such like. A shiny mobile of silvery fish had twirled above a brand-new crib and in the hallway had stood an old-fashioned pram. He had looked out of the window at the seemingly endless green grass of the Common and his heart had clenched with pain as he acknowledged his exclusion. And yet pride stopped him from showing it. He had given a cool shake of his head when she had offered him tea, citing a meeting in the city as the reason why.

She had told him she would be fair and that he could have paternal visiting rights as often as he liked and he believed her, but the idea of living without his son made his heart clench with pain. And yet the thought of an ugly legal battle for their baby had suddenly seemed all wrong.

Why?

Why?

He slept badly—something which was becoming a habit—and he was already waiting when Keeley arrived at the hospital, failing to hide the shock on her face when she saw him.

'Ariston!' Her cheeks went pink. 'You're early!'

'And?'

She looked as if she wanted to say something more but smiled instead, except that, as smiles went, it didn't look terribly convincing. Her mouth seemed strained but he thought he'd never seen her looking more beautiful, in a green velvet coat which matched her eyes and her fair hair hanging over one shoulder in a thick plait.

'Shall we go up to the scanning room?' she said.

'As you wish,' he growled.

The appointment couldn't have gone better. The radiographer smiled and pointed out things which didn't really need pointing out—even to Ariston's untutored eye. The rapidly beating little heart and the thumb which was jammed into a monochrome mouth. He could feel the salt taste of unwanted tears in the back of his throat and was glad that Keeley was busy wiping jelly from her stomach, giving him enough time to compose himself.

And when they emerged into the quiet London street it felt as if he had stepped into another world.

'Would you like lunch?' he questioned formally.

'I…no, thank you.'

'Coffee, then?'

She looked as if she wanted to say something important but although she had opened her lips, she quickly closed them again and shook her head. 'No, thanks. It's very kind of you but I'm off coffee at the moment and I'm…tired. I'd rather get home if it's all the same with you.'

'I'll have my driver drop you off.'

'No, honestly, Ariston. I'll get the bus or the Tube. It's no bother.'

'I'm not having you struggling across London on public transport in your condition. I will have my driver drop you off,' he repeated in a flat tone which didn't quite disguise his growing irritation. 'Don't worry, Keeley. I'll take a cab. I wouldn't dream of subjecting you to any more of my company since you clearly find the prospect so unappealing. Here. Get in.'

He pulled open the door of the limousine which Keeley hadn't even noticed and which had drawn to a smooth and noiseless halt beside them. He was watching her as she slid onto the back seat, the scent of leather and luxury seeming poignantly familiar as she stared into Ariston's blue eyes—those beautiful blue eyes which she had missed so much. Her mouth dried. Should she tell him to come round some time? Would that send out the wrong message—or maybe the real message—that it wasn't just his eyes she had missed?

'Ariston,' she began, but he had closed the car door and given an almost imperceptible nod to his driver as the powerful machine pulled away.

And Keeley turned round, slightly ungainly with her baby bump, wanting to catch a glimpse of his face as the car pulled away. Was she hoping for one of those movie endings, where she would surprise a look of longing on *his* face and she could yell at the driver to stop the car, and...

But he was walking away, striding purposefully towards a black cab which had just switched off its yellow light, and Keeley turned away, biting her lip as the limousine took her southwest, towards Wimbledon.

She was doing the right thing. She was. She kept telling herself that over and over. Why sit through a torturous lunch or even a cup of coffee when Ariston had a face like dark granite? He didn't love her and he never could. He was an unreasonably jealous and controlling man. He might have the power to turn her to jelly whenever he so much as looked at her but he was all the things she despised.

So how come she still wanted him with a longing which sometimes left her breathless with regret for what could never be?

And she was doing this for their baby, she reminded herself. Building respect between them and forging a relationship which would demonstrate what two adults could achieve if they only put their minds to it.

The journey to her cottage took for ever and in truth it would have been quicker getting the train, but the moment she walked up the path to her little house she could feel a slight lifting of her mood. Wimbledon Common had been one of those places she'd always drooled about when she'd lived in New Malden. She used to take the bus there on her day off. It had a villagey feel and a pond, plus lots of lovely little shops and restaurants. She'd seen other pregnant mothers giving her cautious smiles when she was out and about and she wanted to reach out and make friends, but something was holding her back. She shut the front door with a bang. She didn't want to let anyone close because then she would have to explain her circumstances and tell them that her brief marriage was over. Because if she admitted it to someone else, then she would have to accept it was true.

And she didn't want it to be true, she realised. She wanted...

She bit her lip as she batted the dark thoughts away. She didn't dare express what she wanted, not even to herself. All she knew was that she couldn't go back to that old way of living. Of feeling like a pampered doll in someone else's life. A decorative asset to be brought out whenever the situation merited it. She wanted to *connect* with the real world—not sit in her gilded penthouse and look down on it. And most of all she wanted a man who wouldn't make out that feelings were like poison—and you should avoid them whenever possible.

She lit a fire in the grate and had just made a pot

of tea when there was a ring on the bell. She peered through the peephole, shocked to see Ariston standing on her doorstep, his hands shoved deep in the pockets of his trousers, his face a dark glower. She pulled open the door and there he was, his black hair ruffled by the October wind and his jaw all shadowed.

Her heart missed a beat. 'Ariston,' she said, wondering if he could hear the slight quaver in her voice. 'What…what are you doing here?'

His shuttered features looked forbidding. 'Can I come in?'

She hesitated for only a moment before stepping aside to let him pass. 'Of course.'

She wasn't going to do that thing of offering him tea—of pretending this was some kind of social call. There wasn't going to be any of that fake stuff which just wasted time and meant nothing. She would hear him out and then he would go. But a shiver of apprehension whispered over her because an impromptu visit like this didn't bode well—not when his expression was so serious and so *brooding*. Had he decided he was being too soft with her and now that she was showing no signs of moving back, he was going to retaliate? Maybe instruct his lawyers to reduce the generous amount of income she was receiving—to shock her into seeing sense. Was he going to starve her out to make her come back to him? It was an unpalatable thought until she thought of one which was even worse.

That he didn't want her back.

Pain and panic rushed through her like a hot, fierce tide. What if he'd decided that life was easier without a wife who was constantly nagging him because he stayed late at the office? If he'd decided he'd had enough of domesticity and wanted to get back on the party scene. That she had been right all along and the marriage simply wasn't working.

'What do you want, Ariston?' she said, in a low voice. 'Why are you here?'

Ariston stared at her and the trilingual fluency of a lifetime suddenly deserted him. On the way here he'd worked out exactly what he was going to say to her but all the words seemed to have flown straight out of his head. But he knew what he wanted, didn't he? He was a man who was skilled in the art of negotiation. So wasn't it time to go all out and get it?

'I'm going to reduce my hours,' he said.

She looked taken aback, but she nodded. 'Okay.'

'Because I realise that you're right.' He rubbed his fingers over the faint stubble of his chin as if only just realising he'd forgotten to shave that morning. 'I've been working too hard.'

He looked at her expectantly, waiting for the praise which such a magnanimous gesture surely merited and for her to fling herself into his arms to thank him. But she didn't. She didn't move. She just stood there with her green eyes wary and her pale hair glowing in the thin autumn light which was streaming through the window.

'And your point is, what?' she questioned.

'That we'll spend more time together. Obviously.'

She gave an odd smile. 'So what has brought about this sudden revelation?'

He frowned, because her reaction was not what he had imagined it would be. 'I allowed myself to accept that the Kavakos company is in the black and is likely to stay that way for the foreseeable future,' he said slowly.

She screwed up her nose. 'And hasn't it always been?'

Raking his fingers back through his hair, he shook his head. 'No. I think I told you that when my father died, I discovered he'd blown most of the family fortune. For a while it was touch and go whether or not we'd make it. Suddenly I was looking into a big black hole where the future used to be and I had so many people relying on me. Not just Pavlos but all the staff we employed. People on Lasia whose livelihood depended on our success. People in cities all over the world.' He sucked in a deep breath. 'That's why I put the time in—long hours, every day, way past midnight. It took everything I possessed to turn things around and get the company back on an even keel.'

'But that was then, and this is now   and Kavakos is arguably the biggest shipping company in the world.'

He nodded. 'I know that. But hard work got to be such a habit that I let it take me over. And I'm not going to do that any more. I'm going to spend less time at the office and more time at home. With you.' He looked at her. 'That's all.'

The silence which followed seemed to go on and on and when she spoke her voice was trembling.

'But that's not all, Ariston,' she said. 'The reason you work so hard isn't because you've developed some kind of *habit* you can't break or because secretly you live in fear that all your profits are going to disappear overnight. It's because at work you're the one in charge and what you say goes. And you like to be in control, don't you? Work has always provided you with an escape route. It's there for the taking when your wife wants to get too close or tries to talk about stuff you don't want to talk about.'

'Are you listening to a word I've just said?' he demanded. 'I've told you I'll reduce my hours, if that's what it takes to get you back.'

'But don't you realise?' she whispered. 'That's not enough.'

'Not *enough*?' he echoed, his blue eyes laced with confusion. 'What else do you want from me, Keeley?'

And here it was, the question she'd wanted him to ask ever since he had carried her to their bedroom on their wedding night. A no-holds-barred question which would make her vulnerable to so much potential pain if she answered it honestly.

Did she dare?

Could she dare not to?

She'd once vowed never to put herself in a position where she could be rejected again, but that was a vow she'd made when she'd been hurt and humbled. All these years later she was a grown woman who would soon have a baby of her own. And it all boiled down to whether she had the courage to put her pride and her fears aside and to reach out for the one thing she wanted.

'I want your trust,' she said simply. 'I want you to believe me when I tell you things and to stop imagining the worst. I want you to stop trying to control me and let me have the freedom to be myself. I want to stop feeling as if I'm swimming against the tide whenever I try to get close to you. I want ours to be a marriage which *works*—but only if we're both prepared to work at it. I want us to be equals, Ariston. True equals.'

His eyes narrowed as he nodded his head. 'You sound like you've given this some thought.'

'Oh, I've given it plenty,' she said truthfully. 'Only I wasn't sure if I'd ever get the chance to say it.'

There was another silence and the haunted expression on his face tore at Keeley's heartstrings for she saw her own fears and insecurities reflected there. It made her want to go to him and hug him tightly—to offer him her strength and to feel his. But she said nothing. Nothing which would break the spell or the hope that he might just reveal what was hidden in his heart, instead of trying to blot it out and hide it away, the way he normally did. Because that was the only way they could go forward, she realised. If they both were honest enough to let the truth shine through.

'I didn't want to let you close because I sensed danger—the kind of danger I didn't know how to handle,' he said at last. 'I'd spent years perfecting an emotional control which enabled me to pick up the pieces and care for Pavlos when our mother left. A control which kept the world at a safe distance. A control which enabled me to keep all the balls spinning in the air. I was so busy protecting my brother and safeguarding his future, that I didn't have time for anything else. I didn't want anything else. And then I met you and suddenly everything changed. You started to get close. You drew me in, no matter how hard I tried to fight against it, and I recognised that you had the power to hurt me, Keeley.'

'But I don't want to hurt you, Ariston,' she said. 'I am not your mother and you can't judge all women by her standards. I want to be there for you—in every way. Won't you let me do that?'

'I don't think I have a choice,' he admitted huskily. 'Because my life has been hell without you. My apartment and my life are empty when you aren't in them, Keeley. Because you speak the truth to me in a way which is sometimes painful to hear—but out of that pain has grown the certainty that I love you. That perhaps I've always loved you—and I want to go on loving you for the rest of my life.'

And suddenly she could hold out no longer and crossed the room as quickly as her pregnant shape would allow. She went straight into his arms and at last he was holding her tightly and she closed her eyes against the sudden prick of tears.

'Keeley,' he whispered, his mouth pressed hard against her cheek. 'Oh, Keeley. I've been dishonest with myself—right from the start. I felt the thunderbolt the first time I set eyes on you and I'd never felt that way about a woman before. I told myself you were too young—way too young—but then I kissed you and you blew my world apart.' He pulled away and stroked an unsteady finger over her trembling lips. 'It was easier to convince myself that I despised you. To tell myself you were cut from the same cloth as your mother, and that I only wanted sex with you to extinguish the burning hunger inside of me. But you just kept igniting the flames. When you became pregnant—a part of me was exultant. I couldn't decide if it was destiny or fate I needed to thank for a reason to stay close to you. But then came the reality. And the way you made me feel was bigger than anything I've ever felt before. It felt...'

'Scary,' she finished, pulling back a little so that she could gaze deep into his eyes. 'I know. Scary for me, too. Because love is precious and rare and most of us don't know how to handle it, especially when we've grown up without it. But we're bright people, Ariston. We both know what we don't want—broken homes and lost children and bitter wounds which can never be completely healed. I just want to love you and our baby and to create a happy family life. Don't you want that too?'

Briefly, Ariston closed his eyes and when he opened them she was still there, just as she always would be. Because some things you just knew, if only you would let your defences down long enough for instinct to take over. And instinct told him that Keeley Kavakos would always love him, though maybe not quite as much as he loved her.

He pulled her closer, his breath warm against her skin. 'Can we please go to bed so we can plan our future?' he questioned urgently.

'Oh, Ariston.' She rose on tiptoe to wind her arms around his neck, and he could hear the relief which tinged her breathless sigh. 'I thought you'd never ask.'

EPILOGUE

'So, HOW ARE you feeling, my clever and very beautiful wife?'

Keeley lifted her gaze from the tiny black head which was cradled against her breast, to find the bright blue eyes of her husband trained on her.

How was she feeling? Tough question. How could words possibly convey the million sentiments which had rushed through her during a long labour, and which had ended just an hour ago with the birth of their son? Joy, contentment and disbelief were all there, that was for sure—along with a savage determination that she would love and protect their new baby with every fibre of her being. Baby Timon. Timon Pavlos Kavakos. She smiled as she traced a feather-light fingertip over his perfect, olive-skinned cheek.

'I feel like the luckiest woman in the world,' she said simply.

Ariston nodded. He didn't want to contradict her at such a time, but if luck was being handed out—then surely he was its biggest recipient? Watching Keeley go through labour had been something which had taught him the true meaning of powerlessness and silently he had cursed that he was unable to bear or share her pain with her. Yet hadn't it been yet another demonstration of his wife's formidable strength—to watch her cope so beautifully with each increasing contraction? A wife who was planning to join him in the family business, just as soon as the time was right. He remembered her reaction when he'd first put the idea to her and his tender smile in response to her disbelieving joy. But why wouldn't he want his capable and very able wife working beside him, with hours which would suit her and their son? Why wouldn't he want to enjoy her company as much as possible, especially since her command of Greek was getting better by the day?

But she'd told him that these days she studied his language with a passion born from wanting to fit in and not because she was terrified of being left out. Because she was determined to speak the same language as their child. And because family was more important than anything else. A fact which had been drummed home by the sudden death of her mother, a death which in truth had filled Keeley with a sad kind of gratitude, because Vivienne Turner was at peace at last. And it had focussed their minds on the things which mattered. They had decided to make their home on Lasia—on that exquisite paradise of a place, with its green mountains and sapphire sea and skies which were endlessly blue.

Ariston thought how beautiful she looked lying there, still a little pale and exhausted after her long labour, her blonde hair lying damply against her cheeks as she smiled up at him trustingly. 'Would you like to hold your son now?' she whispered.

A lump instantly constricted his throat. It was what he'd been waiting for. In fact, it felt as if he'd been waiting for this moment all his life. A little gingerly at first, Ariston took the sleeping bundle from her, and as he bent to kiss the baby's jet-black hair a fierce wave of love rushed over him. He was used to holding babies because he used to hold Pavlos most of the time—but this felt different. Very different. This child was *his* flesh. And Keeley's. Timon. The pounding of his heart was almost deafening and the lump in his throat was making speech difficult, but somehow he got the words out as he looked into the tear-filled eyes of his wife.

'Efkaristo,' he said softly.

'Thanks for what?' she questioned shakily as he put his free arm tightly around her shoulders and drew her close.

'For my son, for your love—and for giving me a life beyond my wildest dreams. How about that for starters, *koukla mou*?'

She was trying to blink them away but the tears of joy just kept rolling down her cheeks and Ariston smiled as he kissed each one away, while their son slept contentedly in his arms.

* * * * *

If you enjoyed
THE PREGNANT KAVAKOS BRIDE
why not explore these other
ONE NIGHT WITH CONSEQUENCES
themed stories?

THE GUARDIAN'S VIRGIN WARD
by Caitlin Crews
A CHILD CLAIMED BY GOLD
by Rachael Thomas
THE CONSEQUENCE OF HIS VENGEANCE
by Jennie Lucas
SECRETS OF A BILLIONAIRE'S MISTRESS
by Sharon Kendrick
THE BOSS'S NINE-MONTH NEGOTIATION
by Maya Blake

Available now!

Join Britain's BIGGEST Romance Book Club

50% OFF your first parcel

- **EXCLUSIVE offers** every month

- **FREE delivery direct** to your door

- **NEVER MISS a title**

- **EARN Bonus Book** points

Call Customer Services
0844 844 1358*

or visit
millsandboon.co.uk/subscriptions

* This call will cost you 7 pence per minute plus your phone company's price per minute access charge.

CB3